Mogini

An 18th Century Adventure

Moginie
An 18ᵗʰ Century Adventure

L'ILLUSTRE PAISAN ou Memoires et Avantures de Daniel Moginié. Ecrit & adressé par lui même à son Frère François, son Légataire. 1754

Translated and with an introduction by Laurence Cook

"... the manners of mankind do not differ so widely as our voyage writers would make us believe. Perhaps it would be more entertaining to add a few surprising customs of my own invention, but nothing seems to me so agreeable as truth, and I believe nothing so acceptable to you."[1]

MMIV

© Copyright 2004 Laurence Cook. All rights reserved.

No part of this publication may be reproduced, stored in a retrieval system, or transmitted, in any form or by any means, electronic, mechanical, photocopying, recording, or otherwise, without the written prior permission of the author.

Printed in Victoria, Canada

Note for Librarians: a cataloguing record for this book that includes Dewey Classification and US Library of Congress numbers is available from the National Library of Canada. The complete cataloguing record can be obtained from the National Library's online database at:
www.nlc-bnc.ca/amicus/index-e.html
ISBN 1-4120-2677-6

TRAFFORD

This book was published on-demand in cooperation with Trafford Publishing. On-demand publishing is a unique process and service of making a book available for retail sale to the public taking advantage of on-demand manufacturing and Internet marketing. On-demand publishing includes promotions, retail sales, manufacturing, order fulfilment, accounting and collecting royalties on behalf of the author.

Suite 6E, 2333 Government St., Victoria, B.C. V8T 4P4, CANADA
Phone 250-383-6864   Toll-free 1-888-232-4444 (Canada & US)
Fax 250-383-6804   E-mail sales@trafford.com   Web site www.trafford.com
TRAFFORD PUBLISHING IS A DIVISION OF TRAFFORD HOLDINGS LTD
Trafford Catalogue #04-0505   www.trafford.com/robots/04-0505.html

13   12   11   10   9   8   7   6   5   4   3   2

CONTENTS

INTRODUCTION

The book and its context	1
The London notice of Daniel Moginié's travels	4
Persia in the early 18th century	16
India, Persia and the west at the time of Nadir Shah	39
The role of Maubert de Gouvest	50
The origin of the Moginié parchment	60
The English connection	68
Notes and references	82

THE MEMOIR OF DANIEL MOGINIÉ

Part 1	90
Part 2	131

INTRODUCTION

ᛈ The book and its context

The autobiography of Daniel Moginié, a Swiss adventurer, was first published in 1754 under the title l'Illustre Paisan.[2] In it his career takes many turns. Daniel leaves Switzerland as a young man to travel to the Netherlands Indies and from there to Persia where he participates in the civil unrest, successively helping the Afghans, the reigning Shah and the usurper Nadir Shah. On Nadir's behalf he fights the Turks and undertakes a mission to Constantinople. Falling from favour he escapes to his former friends in Kandahar. There he defends the city against Nadir until another escape, this time to India. He serves the Moghul Muhammad Shah, and fights the Persians in the Punjab. Nadir captures Delhi, eventually to withdraw to Persia. Daniel survives as a powerful and titled supporter of the Moghul and marries one of his daughters. Soon illness overtakes him, and he dies longing for a reunion with his younger brother François whom he last saw in the Netherlands. This is a personal account of an exciting life, but since our hero takes part in so many pivotal events, it provides the reader with a review of the recent history of a region in which Europe had an increasing interest.

The preface to the 1754 book contains correspondence stating that Daniel and his brother became convinced of their nobility after finding a genealogy which shows them descended from Iranian kings. There are other letters concerning an attempt to contact the brother, now in London, so that he may travel to India to claim Daniel's inheritance. Although the two brothers certainly existed, it is uncertain that they really experienced all the events described. The book, though not the principal character in it, may be the invention of another writer.

Here is a mystery story without a neat solution. Earlier writers have discussed the circumstances of the production of *l'Illustre Paisan* and have not resolved the inconsistencies. Evidence has been checked by me (and usually found wanting) and a possible pirated source for some of the text is suggested. It seems likely that the book was put into production by J-H. Maubert de Gouvest, who pursued his living writing in French outside the borders of France. He resided for a time in the region where Daniel was born, and had political reasons for portraying the kind of life he lived. Our hero was conceived by someone, even if his life is embroidered by fiction. Either his adventures really occurred or they were worth inventing.

The clichés in the text, most of them at any rate, are intentional. Daniel himself is a stereotype, surrounded by romantic cutouts. His story is cliché enough to be the work of an average eighteenth century novelist. His adventures reflect the lives of thousands of young men of the time, who left their homes in Europe to change the course of history, to become Scottish Generals in Russia, French army commanders to Indian princes, a Greek ruler of Thailand, Swiss, Dutch, Latvians, Scandinavians, Germans who were mercenaries all over the world in other peoples' wars. The Portuguese, whose star had risen centuries earlier, were now beached in the Indies in the shadows of their former power, and learning to accept their fate. Portuguese headstones in Malindi and Goa are testimonies to aristocrats who lived and died in the east never seeing their mother country; in the Bay of Bengal they treated with the local rulers, lived by harrying the shipping in the Sundarbans and were spoken of contemptuously by the British and Dutch as pirates - these people crop up repeatedly as the backbone of the European presence in the east - the sappers, engineers and artillerymen of the Persian and Indian regiments. Though he views himself in a special light, Daniel resembles them - a solitary visitor making his way in a rich, strange and dangerous environment. He is a perpetual bluffer. With every confidence trick he becomes further enmeshed in self-deception; every success is a credit to his enterprise, every setback the result of an accident or a fit of jealousy on the part of another. What we read is not the calculated narrative of an imposter, neither is it the testimony of the natural-born aristocrat retrieving his fortunes in a distant land. It is a muddle. Every situation in which he finds himself contains hope and consequences for the next, not far off. The final goal is ill-defined and never to be realized. Despite the exoticism of the locations and the horrific experiences of war, the story is ordinary and for that reason something to which we can relate.

The book had some success when it came out. There was a London edition published in 1754 and one from Frankfurt in 1755. In 1761 it appeared again in Lausanne, nominally from another publisher. A German translation was published in Berne in 1755. These editions reflect European interest in the unfamiliar but powerful countries to the east, their current state and products and the prospects for trade or military conquest. Attitudes came before acquisitions. At this time and for a century before, there was a deeply embedded interaction between western Asia and Europe. Each side was curious about the other and learned from the exchange.

In the 19th century colonial activity tended to penetrate from the coasts and up rivers, while responses to the colonized countries changed. The story of Daniel resurfaced in two popular British journals in the 1860s. The middle class readership had a different taste for the east, creating what has become known disparagingly as orientalism. Two historical reprints of the French original have since appeared, one from 1912, the other in 1988.³ In the following pages the Victorian viewpoint sets the scene.

❧ The London notice of Daniel Moginié's travels

An anonymous article published in 1864 in *Chambers's Journal* begins as follows: ⁴

> In a London journal, dated the 18th of October 1750, the following extraordinary advertisement may be seen, signed by Colonel du Perron, in the service of the Great Mogul:
> This is to inform Francis Moginié, of the canton of Berne, Switzerland, now supposed to be in England, that his deceased elder brother, Daniel Moginié, bore the title of Prince of Didon and Indus, was chamberlain and generalissimo to the Great Mogul. He married a rich princess, who died childless before her husband, and his property is valued at more than two hundred thousand louis-d'or. His wealth and titles devolve upon his brother Francis, whom he has made his sole legatee. I have seen his will, and brought with me his watch, which I will give up to none but Francis Moginié. I can be addressed at the Hôtel de l'Agneau, at Liege, or at the post-office, Frankfort-on-the-Maine, up to April next, where he has only to enquire for Colonel du Perron.

The story continues because the advertisement actually reached the notice of the surviving brother, by this time keeping a little public house in London. He immediately wrote to the Colonel to obtain further details. Daniel had died in May 1749, his possessions going to the Emperor, who would only release them to a properly authenticated heir. As support the Colonel had brought with him the travelling watch, a massive gold medal presented for service to the Emperor and an engraved topaz seal that Francis would recognise as belonging to the family in Switzerland.

Francis joined the Colonel in France, where he received these evidences, went to Berne to obtain copies of his own and his brother's baptismal registers, and set out for India. Arriving at the English Factory in Surat, north of Bombay, he was made welcome by Mr Gogham, one of the senior merchants. In due time he passed on to Agra, to be lodged by the Nabob in great luxury with a suite of thirty servants to attend to his needs. After many days of waiting he was granted an audience with this gentleman, and received the offer of his brother's posts. He possessed much more modest accomplishments and expectations than his brother, however, and on declining was given instead a sum of money amounting to a hundred thousand rupees and a large portfolio containing a manuscript written in French. This was Daniel's autobiography, bequeathed to his brother, or, should that not prove possible after a lapse of five years, to his relatives in Switzerland via the French ambassador at Constantinople. We hear little more of Francis in India, and it is probable that he never returned to his family in London.

The brothers were born in Switzerland. How was it that one was to spend at least part of his life in India and the other in England? On this subject the writer has something to say. The family came from the village of Chesalles-sur-Moudon in a French speaking canton of Switzerland not far from Lausanne, where the name Moginier is still to be found. Although of modest means they lived in a large old house. According to the deeds it had once been a chateau, though the greater part was now ruined. A nearby manor house once belonged to a great uncle and the family was proud of its aristocratic background. Once, when Daniel was seventeen, the brothers were at a family gathering after one of their cousins had been beaten by a nobleman, who had caught him hunting in his forests. There were bitter complaints about this affront and talk of the opulent days and gentlemanly pursuits of the past. One of the party suggested that, like their clothes, the title was so old that it was thoroughly worn out. Their father reminded them that traditionally each generation of the family asked the next to preserve the house, and believed that the title to their inheritance was hidden within its walls.

With his head full of wine, nobility and grandeur, Daniel retired to bed and soon began to dream of treasure. Rousing his brother, he told him what he had dreamt, and they decided to search the building at a place where a large black stone had been embedded in the masonry. When their father had departed to market they went to this spot and attacked the stone with a heavy hammer. It soon gave way, revealing a cavity in which was a cast-iron box. Instead of the gold and diamonds they hoped to find, it contained nothing but a parchment roll, covered with writing in strange characters. What should they do next? They had heard accounts of a notable scholar in nearby Lausanne, so they walked over to beg for an interview. Eventually he received them, examined the manuscript and gave his opinion. It was a genealogy written in an obscure form of Arabic characters which he could not read. If they wished, he would buy it. If they preferred to keep it, the only man in Europe who could possibly provide a translation was to be found at Leiden in the Netherlands.

Excited by this revelation but penniless, Daniel informed his father that he wished to join the regiment of Captain Stürler, just then being raised in Berne for service in Holland. His father was delighted with this decision and offered his blessing and some coins to start him on his way. When he was enrolled, Daniel was provided with another sum of money for his uniform and sent on to Utrecht to join his fellow recruits. We learn nothing of how Francis managed it, but soon he too was in Utrecht, where he became servant to Mr Dillington, an English gentleman. This engagement must have been the first step on the path which led him to London, eventually to be sought by Col. du Perron.   The brothers then set out to find the person who could unravel the mystery of the hidden parchment. At first they were disappointed. The professor in Leiden to whom they had been referred was inclined to send them away, but hearing how far they had travelled he looked at the document, declared it to be a fable in the Arab style but not in Arabic and admitted that he could not decipher it. "Go to Amsterdam," he said, "and seek out Mr Kalb, who used to be Commandant of Malacca and member of the council of Batavia. He is the only man, so far as I know, who can give you any information."

The brothers managed to continue their journey despite their other commitments, and in Amsterdam they met with more success. Mr Kalb was to become Daniel's patron and provide his opportunity to travel in the east. Having determined that the document was written in "Malay or primitive Indian" he spent some days translating it. What he then had to tell Daniel is of sufficient importance to report in full.

> "Permit me to acknowledge you as one of the first gentlemen in the world; the Jews only can boast a descent more ancient than yours. Your ancestors were kings before the reign of Cyrus, more than two thousand years ago. This manuscript,

which is a genealogy, is well followed up from Amorgines, king of Saces, to Boghud Amorgines, son-in-law of Bojas Arsacides, who lived in obscurity on the banks of the Caspian Sea during the reign of the califs. In the year 928, the Bojacides, who descended through the second kings of Persia from Darius son of Hystaspes, formed a party, and dethroned the calif, one of them named Amarxes taking his place. His posterity reigned until 1062, when the barbarians, who are not otherwise designated, overran Persia; Sapor Amorgines being then the chief of your family, which is called the Royal Family. He had five sons; this book only speaks of the third, who, after a great battle lost by Amelkrem, the last of the Bojacide kings, fled into the Caucasus, and thence to Constantinople. Not receiving the attention he expected from this court, he passed on to Rome, where he married. He was still in possession of some jewels, the wreck of his former fortune, and by the sale of these, he determined to purchase a small estate in a country where nothing should interfere with the obscure tranquillity which seemed most suitable to his misfortunes; and for this purpose he settled in the lovely Canton of Vaud, then forming a part of the kingdom of Savoy. Having been baptised at Rome, he received the name of Peter. This book is written by him; he has dated it 1069 AD., the sixth of the ruin of the empire of the Bojacides, 1617 since the battle fought against Cyrus."

After that, the article goes on to describe Daniel's subsequent adventures, leading ultimately to India, the wealth of Golconda, and an early grave. These sonorous phrases belong to the narrator, who nowhere reveals the source of his material. In fact the text is, almost word for word, including the advertisement, letters from India and story of the parchment, the account presented in a book published in 1754 by Pierre Verney of Lausanne. It is entitled: L'ILLUSTRE PAISAN OU MEMOIRES ET AVANTURES DE DANIEL MOGINIÉ, Natif au Village de Chézales, au Canton de Berne, Baillage de Moudon, mort, à Agra, le 22. de Mai 1749. agé de 39 ans; Omrah de la Ire Classe, Commandant de la Seconde Garde Mogole, grand Portier du Palais de l'Empereur, & Gouveneur du Palngëab, Où se trouvent plusiers Particularités Anecdotes des dernières Révolutions de la Perse & de l'Indostan, & du Règne de Thamas-Kouli-Kan. Ecrit & adressé par lui même à son Frère François, son Légataire.[5]

By implication this is autobiography, with notes added, although the dedication at the front is signed M. de G. No details explain who bore these initials. There is no indication how the text passed from the hands of Francis to the publisher. Francis soon disappears from the scene. So far as the book is concerned he is no more than a literary device, but he is certainly the founder of a line of Moginies living in England. Is the rest simply a romance? It would be very satisfying to locate some independent evidence for the circumstantial details presented in both book and article, the Stürlers, Kalbs, Dillingtons and Bojacides with which they are packed. A good place to start is the Colonel's advertisement.

If the notice from Colonel du Perron was indeed printed in a London newspaper there is just a chance that a copy exists today. A possible source is the newspaper collection of the British Library, where history is stored undigested, page by page - yesterday, last year, a decade ago, the 1930s, the 19th century. Researchers abstract tiny squeaks of information, each one vivid at the time and surrounded by its own capsule of context, and put them into a broader frame, the general murmur of human enterprise and eccentricity through the ages. To get to the 18th century it is necessary to resort to microfilm. The impression of winding time backwards is insistent.

October 18th was a Thursday in 1750. London was a thriving city, evidently served by numerous newspapers, of which a dozen or more survive in the records.[6] They usually consisted of four sheets costing a penny or tuppence, and dated from Thursday to Saturday, so they really counted as weekly publications. Some kind of agency service existed, since many carried the same news items. There was, for example, a story of the wine in Paris which killed some drinkers and was afterwards found to come from a barrel containing a toad, and the party where a bullet was discharged by mistake, bounced off a wall and the caster of a table leg, but killed nobody. A large sale of pickled herring from Yarmouth was interesting enough to be reported in several papers. Overseas news was sketchy, but some reports came in: thus "According to the last Advices from Persia, the Schah Doub, who has settled his Residence as Ispahan, is like to remain the quiet Possessor, at least of the South West Provinces of that great Kingdom."

Some papers tended to specialize; for example, *The London Gazette* had many notices of bankruptcy and of persons claiming the benefit of an Act lately passed for the Relief of Insolvent Debtors. Another (*The General Advertiser*) had much shipping news, including ship sales "by the Candle at Lloyd's Coffee House in Lombard-Street". There were serial stories then, as in Victorian times, for example, a death cell account of himself by a condemned man executed in 1726, a sort of auto-obituary. Notices of lost items, auctions, and plays were plentiful, and there were many advertisements for new publications. "This Day is published, Written by Henry Fielding, Esq., the Fourth Edition of The Tragedy of

Tragedies; or, The Life and Death of Tom Thumb the Great; With the Annotations of H. Scriblerius Secundus."

Advertisements tended to be quite eccentrically composed, presumably in the words of the advertiser. Daffy's Elixir was a widely advertised cure, although one news report showed that it had failed Daffy himself, for he had unfortunately died. Surprisingly, there was little reference to religion. The *Rambler* consists of a single essay in each issue, while the monthly *Gentleman's Magazine* had quite long instructive articles on antiquities, French grammar, the pangolin from south-east Asia, a new fast carriage recently tested at Newmarket, and so on. The only sport covered was horse racing, with names of horses, their owners and the purse for which they ran.

The items available come from a range of popular newspapers published between the 16th and 20th of October 1750. Nowhere was there a notice by Colonel du Perron, which is not, in itself, surprising. There were many broadsheets, not held by the Library, and we do not know what kind of publication would be most suitable. Francis was a publican, landlord, perhaps, of one of the 207 inns or 447 taverns recorded as existing within the city bounds. The *Innkeeper's Universal Advertiser* sounds the ideal place to look, but all copies for October 18th seem to have suffered the common fate of printed ephemera.

Papers also fed upon themselves, however, as they do today. *The Gentleman's Magazine*, "By Sylvanus Urban, Gent.", for October 1750, had a page headed "Plays at the Theatres, Remarkable Advertisements". The left column bears notices of plays and entertainments at all the major theatres; Henry Fielding is much in evidence. The right is a collection of extracts from other publications, which happened to catch the editor's attention. At the bottom of the page is the following entry.

> Thurs Oct. 18. Advertisement to acquaint *Francis Moginie* from *Berne* in *Switzerland*, that his eldest brother, who was called prince *Didon* and *Indus*, and was become lord chamberlain and generalissimo of the Mogul's army, and had married a rich princess (who dyed before him without issue) dyed in 1749, leaving an estate of 200,000 louis d'or's. These two brothers, it seems, left *Switzerland* when one of them was about 15, and the other about 16 years of age, having both dreamed, 2 nights before their departure, that a book of their family was buried in the wall of one of their country houses: upon which they searched and found it, after it had been hid 1000 years.

That is all. There is no indication where this item first appeared, or how it managed to make the October issue if first published on the 18th. It also seems curious that the Colonel included in his first advertisement details of the ages of the brothers or their dreams. Francis was undoubtedly in London at the time. Parish registers and other records show that he married a woman called Elizabeth Kemp at St Anne, Soho in 1742. They had four children who died young and a son, John George, born in 1746, who survived to marry and continue the line. Letters providing some details of the life of Francis, were published in Switzerland in 1751.[7] We might be tempted to think the author of the entry in *The Gentleman's Magazine* had read *l'Illustre Paisan*, but that book will only appear four years later, at Lausanne. For further information we must go to it.

After recounting the details covered here, Daniel takes us on his journey overseas. He departed from Texel in the Netherlands with Mr Kalb on 27th June 1728, when he was eighteen, travelling on a

Company vessel bound for Batavia. The trading company involved was the Dutch East India Company, or Vereenigde Oost-indische Compagnie (VOC). It had received a charter from the States-general of the Netherlands at the beginning of the 17th Century, which gave it powers to enlist personnel, built fortresses, wage war, and conclude treaties in Asia. Sailings from the Netherlands are recorded, and have been reprinted, so that one can easily inspect the records for 1728. Between the 20th May and 28th October, 1728 only three boats set out from Texel.[8] The first was the Buis, commanded by Captain Dirk Dol, 600 tons, which left on 22nd June, arriving at the Cape on 8th January 1729, and departing from there on 28th February to reach Batavia by 16th May. No passengers are recorded, which does not mean there definitely were none, but four craftsmen embarked, one dying on the way. This boat stopped at Sao Thomé for a week. On the 23rd June the yacht Slot Aldegonde, Captain Gillis Oudemans, 580 tons, set off, arriving at the Cape on 4th November and departing again on 19th December. Its tally list includes only seafarers and soldiers. On the same day the Stad Leiden, a larger boat of 1140 tons, Captain Wouter van Dijk, also left, arriving at the Cape 21st October, departing from there 18th November and reaching Batavia on 9th February 1729. Three passengers were embarked and none is recorded as dying, the fate suffered by Mr Kalb before reaching the Cape of Good Hope. None of the descriptions quite fits the Moginié version, but they very nearly do, the last being the most likely. Dying *en voyage* was quite common at the time. For all sailings in 1728, none of the 26 recorded passengers died, but 404 seafarers from the total of 4782 who manned them, perished on the way.

The VOC was flourishing at this time and there were trading stations and bases from the Persian Gulf down the west coast of India, the Peninsula, Ceylon, Bengal and the Sunda islands. Boats were built at Malacca to carry Chinese porcelain for the European market and there was a massive trade in spices. The Company maintained a very restrictive monopoly and kept its employees on low wages, so that the rich were those who indulged in illicit trade on their own account. One of the sources the English reader had for information on these places was a work by William Guthrie, much consulted in Britain in the 18th century.[9] Guthrie was a jobbing writer, one of whose activities was to report and arrange Parliamentary debates for the *Gentleman's Magazine*, a sort of precursor to Hansard, and he wrote a number of histories. "He has no great regular fund of knowledge, but by reading so long and writing so long he has no doubt picked up a good deal", said Johnson of him, to Boswell. At all events, the Dutch Indies impressed him.

> The greatest part of Java belongs to the Dutch, who have here erected a kind of commercial monarchy, the capital of which is Batavia, a noble and populous city, lying in the latitude of six degrees south, at the mouth of the river Jucata, and furnished with one of the finest harbours in the world. The town itself is built in the manner of those in Holland, and is about a league and a half in circumference, with five gates, and surrounded by regular fortifications; but its suburbs are said to be ten times more populous than itself. The government here is a mixture of Eastern magnificence and European police, and held by the Dutch governor-general of the Indies. When he appears abroad, he is attended by his guards and officers, and with a splendour superior to that of any European potentate, excepting upon solemn occasions. The city is as beautiful as it is strong, and its fine canals, bridges and avenues, render it a most agreeable residence.

The description of it, its government, and public edifices, have employed whole volumes.

In the first part of his account, Daniel comes over as a delightful personality, to whom everyone takes an almost instant liking. An alternative reading would make him a self-satisfied prig. Some of the setbacks result from his impetuosity, but most are attributed to jealousy on the part of one person or another. The cast, in order of appearance below, have names, occupations and locations. Either they are the circumstantial evidence showing the events to be true, or they have been slipped in to provide an air of verisimilitude. Mr Dillington, an English gentleman or nobleman (he is referred to as *chevalier* in the book) took François into service at Utrecht. The two of them could have travelled immediately to England, but it seems quite as likely that Mr Dillington would be setting out on a tour of Europe and engaged a servant to assist him on his travels. Captain Stürler was a Swiss military man who had raised a troop to fight in the Low Countries. Daniel signs up with him as a means to get to Amsterdam, but he is willingly released when a life of adventure overseas beckons. Stürler actually existed, and documents about his regiment, but they do not include Daniel's name. Mr Kalb is said to be a former Commandant of Malacca, member of Council of Batavia. He likes our hero so much as to give everyone the impression that Daniel is his son. He dies at the Cape of Good Hope in the late summer or autumn of 1728 while travelling to Batavia on board an India Company ship. Mme Kalb lives at Batavia, with her daughter. Her husband's name does not appear in Dutch East India Company records for Malacca. M. Turretaz is a compatriot of Daniel from Orbe, near Chesalles. He had formerly worked for the Company at Batavia, and then as their agent at the Cape. By the time Daniel meets him he owns land there and has a wife and five children. His name does not figure in lists of early Huguenot settlers.[10] Mr Master is a rich old man in Batavia who looks after Daniel when his intended marriage to Mlle. Kalb leads to disaster. M. d'Imberbault is Commandant of the Fort at Malacca, a Frenchman who had spent 25 years as captain of artillery in the service of the Netherlands in Europe. He prepares Daniel for a military career in Persia.

☙ Persia in the early 18th century

The period leading up to Daniel's landing in Persia was one of complete anarchy.[11] The country was rich and powerful, producing many products desirable in Europe. For that reason direct trade with Persia had been developing progressively for more than a century. For the same reason, there were many elements, both within and outside the country, which tended to disrupt the established regimes or to usurp power.

For millennia the region had been prey to waves of conquerors, through the Mongols, the Oghus and Seljuk Turks, the Arabs of the early Moslem conquests, the Greeks of Alexander, back to the establishment of the Persians themselves and beyond. For the events which bear directly on the story it is enough to consider the 18th century, when the important political developments may be traced to Afghanistan, the mountainous region separating Persia from India, which descends on its western side to the plains of Khorasan and Turkestan. Many groups of peoples participated, the Afghans themselves, and various other nations of that country, Turks from central Asia, Arabs, Iranians, including holders of the old Zoroastrian faith, Bakhtiaris, Lurs, Kurds and Armenians, while Georgians, Russians and Ottoman Turks applied pressure to the north and west.

Apart from race and language, there were religious differences; many Afghans and Uzbegs were Sunni while the Persians were Shias.

At the turn of the 18th Century of the Christian era the province of Kandahar, in the south of Afghanistan, had been fought over, lost and regained successively by Uzbegs, Persians and the Moghul Emperors of India. To reinforce his control, when he had it, the Persian Shah Hussain brought in the Georgian prince Gurgin, or Giorgi, who marched there with an army of twenty thousand Persians and Georgians. To consolidate his position, Gurgin removed the hereditary mayor of Kandahar, Mir Wais, and had him sent to the Persian capital Isfahan. This did not have the intended effect, because Mir Wais became a confidante of the Shah. Claiming support from religious leaders in Mecca and from the embassy of Peter the Great of Russia, he persuaded the Shah to send him back to Kandahar. The unwisdom of this move was soon seen when Gurgin was assassinated, Mir Wais reinstated and the Shah forced to treat with him when he threatened vengeance on the heretical, Shia, Persians. Several commanders were sent against him, including a nephew of Gurgin who wished to avenge his murder, but by the time of his death in 1715, Mir Wais was undisputed ruler of Kandahar province. He was succeeded by members of his family, whose power increased.

These setbacks and successes were typical of events in other provinces. To the north the Heratis, assisted by neighbouring Turks, rode into Khorasan. The Shah sent an army of thirty thousand against this Sunni enemy, which, after some successes, was also defeated. Mahmud, son of Mir Wais, advanced into Persia and captured a large swathe of territory to the south of the Great Desert. He was repulsed by the Persian commander Luft Ali Khan and retired to Kandahar, but his chance came again when Luft Ali Khan was dismissed as a result of an intrigue at the Shah's Court. The will of the Persians was reduced by calamity and terror. It suffered from the fact that Shah Hussain was a weak ruler, and from superstitious alarms such as the foreboding caused by an earthquake at Tabriz which gave rise to blood-coloured sunsets.

Mahmud advanced again, until he faced the main Persian force, supported by Arabs and Lurs, near the capital Isfahan. The result was an ignominious defeat for the Persians. A series of pauses and skirmishes followed, in which the Persians recouped some of their losses but did not distinguish themselves. Attempts at negotiation failed and prisoners were massacred on both sides. Isfahan was besieged and gradually worn down, the only hope of reprieve being the sporadic successes of Persian commanders fighting an assortment of peoples in other parts of the land. By 1722, Isfahan could hold out no longer. The streets were full of the dead and dying, food was exhausted and starving people had taken to eating human flesh. The city surrendered, and with this loss, the established dynasty, the Safavids, was near its end. Thamasp Mirza, the third son of the Shah, had been proclaimed heir apparent and continued at large with a body of troops.

Mahmud, with his Afghan confederacy, extended his power over Persia, but as he was doing so he also had to contend with outside forces. By 1722, Peter the Great had triumphed over Sweden, and used the opportunity to push the Russian Empire southwards. He descended the Volga to the Caspian Sea with a fleet and army, reaching Baku by 1723. Russian advances in this theatre were made easier by an agreement reached with the Ottoman Empire. In 1718 the Peace of Passarowitz stabilized Turkey's long frontier with Austria. With Russia there continued to be a dispute over whether some Caucasus tribes should pay tribute to Czar or Sultan. Cossacks were outlaws mainly of Polish and Russian origin in southern Ukraine. They were nominally under the Czar, who used them as a buffer against the Tartars, a splinter group from the Golden Horde which had settled among Goths in the Crimea and along the northern Black Sea. The Turks, for their part, used the Tartars as advance and rearguard to their army when at war. Not unexpectedly, there were unending disputes between Russia and Turkey over these frontier subjects. The Turks wanted loot and also needed to stop Russia controlling the Caspian Sea and advancing into Daghestan. When they saw the turn of events in 1722 they invaded Georgia, and by their conflicting interests these two powers proceeded further to destabilise Persia.

Thamasp made a treaty with the Russians, agreeing to cede part of his territory if they would help displace the Afghans. This was not to be, as Peter was held up by threats from the Turks and loss of supplies in the Caspian. By 1723 Mahmud had suffered a number of setbacks, however, sending his cousin Ashraf back to Kandahar to attend to affairs there. In order to impose his will on Isfahan with a much depleted army, he issued an order condemning all Persians who had served Hussain. Fifteen days of killing ensued, reducing the population to impotence, and incidentally threatening foreign merchant interests, including those of the Dutch and English Companies. Having removed this potential danger, he attacked Shiraz, which was weakened by famine, using a detachment of Sunni Kurds and a Zoroastrian force. Their commander, Zeberdest Khan, took Shiraz in 1724 and marched on to occupy Bandar Abbas. Although successful, this Afghan army was now exhausted and lacking in direction. Mahmud decided to kill all the members of the Safavid dynasty who were in his hands. These included Hussain but not Thamasp, still in the field and constituting a serious threat. Mahmud is reputed to have gone mad at this time, dying in 1725, and Ashraf was recalled to rule in his place.

 The foregoing complex and desolate catalogue of events was matched elsewhere by attacks by the Ottomans who, having concluded their treaty with Russia, conquered the whole of western Persia by 1725, from Armenia through Tabriz and southwards to the Gulf. Historians speak of ten, twenty or thirty thousand soldiers on each side in these battles, with losses to one party or another sometimes being almost as large. Coupled with the mortality preceding the ending of the siege of a city, or following its capitulation, these figures attest both to the inherent abundance of the land and the ruin into which it was falling. Writing a little later, William Guthrie described the capital, Isfahan, and commented on its decline. Isfahan was twelve miles in circumference; at the centre was a Royal Square a third of a mile in length containing an enormous walled royal palace and gardens. There were 160 mosques, 1800 caravanserais, 260 public baths. Fine squares were lined with trees planted to provide shade, and canals brought water which made the city luxuriant and cool. The streets were often crooked and narrow, lined with dwellings which had flat roofs used for idling and gossip by the inhabitants on summer evenings. Before the Afghan attacks Isfahan had contained 650,000 inhabitants, but by 1744 no more than 5000 houses were inhabited.

 Ashraf, who appears to have been an astute leader, now played the religious card against the Ottomans, asking why they, as Sunnis, should join forces with a Christian state to attack another Sunni power, with the probable effect of restoring a Shia Emperor to the throne. This plea, and some military success, resulted in a treaty with the Ottomans concluded in 1727. One flank was thus protected, but Thamasp continued to present a threat. He was established in the north, with a significant military commander called Thamasp Kouli Khan, or Nadir Khan. They marched eastward to Khorasan and Herat, capturing them and establishing a power base. In 1729 Ashraf's Afghans were defeated twice in battle. Ashraf retired with his remaining forces and their families to Isfahan, to withstand another attack. Having realized the position was hopeless, they then withdrew to Shiraz. The armies of Thamasp and Nadir followed them there. After sporadic skirmishes, defections and treachery the Afghans were completely demoralised and the Persians completely victorious. Shah Thamasp received as a gift the head of Ashraf and a large diamond which was found on him, Nadir obtained the right to raise taxes on his own behalf and, this being the year 1730, or 1142 after the Hegira, Daniel landed on the coast to the south of them, hoping to make his fortune.

The arrival of Nadir on the scene had such a profound effect on events in Persia, Afghanistan and India that it is useful to cover the main points of his career, which coincided and supposedly interacted with that of our hero. He was born in 1688 into the family of a peasant in the village of Dastgird in north-eastern Persia. The family belonged to the Afshar tribe, which was probably Turkish, although in that region it is sometimes difficult to determine whether a tribe is Turkish or Mongol. They had migrated to Khorasan over a century earlier and had winter and summer pasturage around the Alahu Akbar mountains. A later biographer suggested that Nadir was born in the castle of Dastgird and provided a heroic past for the Afshars as members of the Oghuz Turkish horde. A yurt is a much more likely birthplace, and his father was probably a minor farmer or camel-driver. When he was still young he entered the service of a chief of the Afshars who was Governor of the town of Abivard. There, he rose to command the guards and become the Governor's son-in-law.

The Governor appears to have died in 1723 leaving his property to Nadir, who went to Meshed and entered service of a leader there. As so often happened in these accounts, the young and aspiring commander fell out with his master, and attempted to kill him, murdering instead two Afshar chiefs who had been supposed to help him in the enterprise. He fled to Abivard, and raised a force which proceeded to pillage and raid in Khorasan, and continued to arrange alliances to fight another local war-lord. Much fighting then ensued, during which he came to the attention of Shah Thamasp, who appointed him deputy governor of Abivard in 1726. Thereafter, he consolidated his position by ousting rivals, to become principal commander and advisor to Thamasp.

After making Nadir ruler of a large part of northern and eastern Persia, Thamasp set out to attack the Turks. This time his efforts met with disaster, however, and in 1732 he was forced to sign a treaty which ceded much of the west to the Ottomans. Outraged by this treaty, or perhaps seeing an opportunity he desired, Nadir vowed to resume the Turkish war. From Herat he issued proclamations threatening the Turks and all those in Persia who refused to join the battle. Accusing Thamasp of cowardice and misconduct, he captured him and sent him as a prisoner to Khorasan, putting his infant son on the throne and proclaiming himself Regent. He then marched across the country to besiege Baghdad, and might have succeeded easily had he not been threatened by a large Turkish force to the north under its leader Topal Osman. The resulting battle he lost, and Baghdad was saved for the Turks. In Constantinople, however, Osman had made an enemy of the Kizlar Aga, otherwise the Chief Black Eunuch, Aga of the House of Felicity and Controller of the Harem. Funds and reinforcements were cut off. In a second battle Nadir was victorious and Osman was killed. The Peace of Baghdad was concluded in

December 1733, to replace the treaty signed by Thamasp. Before leaving Baghdad, Nadir sent the new treaty to Constantinople, with letters for the Turkish Grand Vizier.

The next three years saw a series of engagements, in which the Ottoman forces were subdued, the territories they had so recently captured regained, and the Russians forced to abandon the Caspian provinces. In 1736 the infant Shah died and Nadir urged the Persian ministers of state to choose a new Shah without delay. They did so, judiciously suggesting that he might like to ascend the Throne. He agreed, and was crowned with some pomp, issuing commemorative coins stamped with the words Phoenix of Persia, World-conqueror and Sovereign. In 1737 the World-conqueror set out to retake Kandahar, still in the hands of Hussain, brother of the Mahmud who was fleetingly ruler of Persia. From there, his route took him east of the Hindu Kush to Peshawar and then on to Lahore and Delhi, which he reached in 1739.

It may seem surprising that any European country would find it profitable to trade with one continually rent by war and crossed and re-crossed by pillaging armies, but such seems to be the case. To some extent that is because the region was naturally productive and capable of growing crops unavailable in Europe. Guthrie speaks of the richness of the south where the fertility of the land in corn, fruits, wine and the other luxuries of life was equalled by few countries. Products included senna, rhubarb, dates, oranges, pistachio nuts, melons, cucumbers, and almost all the flowers that were valued in Europe. From some of them, the roses especially, salubrious and odorific waters were extracted and traded. Asa foetida was collected as a plant gum, some white and some black, "but the former is so much valued, that the natives make very rich sauces of it, and sometimes eat it as a rarity." Of manufactured goods, the Persians equalled, if not exceeded, all the manufacturers of the world in silks, woollens, mohair, carpets and leather. Their works in these joined "A fancy, taste, and elegance, to richness, neatness, and show." .... "Their dying excels that of Europe. Their silver and gold laces, and threads, are admirable for preserving their lustre. Their embroideries and horse furniture are not to be equalled, nor are they ignorant of the pottery, and window glass manufactures." Some products were even then becoming exhausted, however. The Gulf of Basra once furnished the great part of Europe and Asia with fine pearls, but not in Guthrie's time.

To some extent, western interest was local diplomacy and power politics carried on in another theatre. The fortunes of the Turks and Persians in Persia were of great significance to the Austrians and Russians, who had borders with the Ottoman Empire. The French allied themselves with the Ottomans in their struggle with the Austrian Empire. The British and Dutch competed on every front for commercial supremacy.

At the Sublime Porte the game was played in diplomatic terms. By the early eighteenth century the power of Venice had declined. The important political players were the consuls of France, Austria and Russia. The envoys of the Austrian Emperor and of the Czar or Czarina, both held the rank of Resident. The Marquis de Villeneuve, Lieutenant-General of Marseilles, the French city which traded with Turkey, was Ambassador to the Sultan. Count Bonneval had been a French general from an early age, then fell out with the French authorities and moved to Vienna, where he reached a high rank in the Imperial army. He quarrelled with the Austrians in their turn, and offered his talents to Turkey. Suffering from gout and wearing a silver plate over an unhealed wound to his stomach, he became a Muslim and trained the Bombardier Corp of the Turkish Army. From this position he actively worked against the interests of Austria.

One game played in Constantinople by these figures concerned the war of succession to the Polish throne. King Augustus II of Poland died in 1733. Austria and Russia backed Frederick, the son of the late King, as his successor. Looking for a candidate who would be subservient to her interests and a threat to the Habsburgs, France supported Stanislas, the father-in-law of Louis XV. War was declared between the French and the Habsburg Emperor. The three countries sent instructions to their envoys in Constantinople as to how they should present the Polish case to the Sultan. Russia needed Frederick in place and feared Turkish support of his rival. Austrians feared a French attack and instructed their Resident to keep a close watch on Bonneval to prevent him suggesting a Turkish attack towards Belgrade. For their part, the French wished to stop a Russian advance into Poland, and sought to induce the Sultan to attack the Russians on their flank.

In Constantinople, the Russian Resident gave the Sultan presents and got an assurance that he would not intervene before the end of the year. Villeneuve sent an attaché to the Tartar Khan in the Crimea, a supporter of Stanislas, persuading him to harass the Russians. The Sultan was not willing to be moved, and Villeneuve concluded that Bonneval was influencing him against the scheme. Bonneval told the other Residents about the French approaches. Vienna and St Petersburg both accused France of making common cause with the infidel and the British and Dutch Ambassadors were instructed to frustrate French efforts.

By 1735 the French had won their war against Austria, and by so doing increased the security of the Ottoman Empire. The Tartar Khan then marched through the Caucasus to attack the Persians from the rear. The following year the Russians attacked Azov, a Turkish fortress which prevented them having a trade route to the Black Sea, and moved on into the Crimea where they temporarily routed the Tartars. Turkey declared war on Russia and the three-cornered relations between Turkey, Persia and Russia changed again. Threats of war between Turkey and various countries of Europe also continued, with Ambassadors and Residents vying with each other to promote their national interests.

These struggles of the three European powers were of minor political interest to England at the time, so funds were restricted. British Ambassadors found themselves promoting both His Majesty's Government and the Levant Company, which paid the greater part of the Ambassador's salary. Edward Wortley Montagu, whose unsuccessful embassy occurred in 1716, received £500 from that source. One holder of the post augmented his salary by mediation between the other powers on a consultancy basis. Another was described as "preoccupied with his debts and his women, habitually drunk and a bore."

In the commercial sphere, Britain had at this time another entrée to Persia which looked to bypass the unrest in eastern Europe so long as the British remained on good terms with Russia. In 1734 a commercial treaty was concluded, that made provision for British merchants to send goods via St Petersburg to Persia or vice versa on payment of 3 per cent duty. Captain John Elton, an "enterprising but indiscreet Englishman", tried to develop this in 1739. He travelled down the Volga and sailed with trading goods to Resht, on the south coast of the Caspian Sea, where he obtained from the Persians a permit to establish a Factory. The Persian capital had moved north to Meshed, and the route avoided both the overland journey from the south and the taxation of goods sent through the Ottoman Empire. Elton published an enthusiastic account of the proposed enterprise in the *Gentleman's Magazine* in 1742. Ships were built to sail the Caspian and by 1743 a Factory was also established at Meshed.

The Europeans were trying to enter a market which was rewarding but volatile, and was already run by skilled and enterprising merchants. About fifty years after this period, Alexander Burnes pointed out that profits as great as forty per cent could be made, but that the risks were correspondingly high.[12] He writes of meeting a merchant at Astrabad who was travelling to Khiva with a consignment of sugar candy. He had purchased it in Tehran and was proceeding by boat along the south Caspian coast, past Cheleken Island to a port near present-day Krasnovodsk. There he would set off across the Kara Kum desert to Khiva, using hired Turcoman camels. This was a practical undertaking because the dangerous Turcoman marauders operated well south of the trade route nearer the Persian border. "What a proof of enterprise is this!" Burnes exclaimed. The sugar had first been brought from China to Bombay. Next it was shipped to Bushire, sent inland to Tehran and from there to the banks of the Caspian. At Khiva it would compete with British sugar from the Caribbean that had been exported to Russia and transported overland. If bulky and relatively cheap commodities could be taken so far and still be profitable then imagine the possibilities for trade in British manufactures along the same routes.

Fifty years before, Elton entered the service of Nadir Shah, and by so doing alarmed the Russians and reduced their willingness to allow Russia to be a conduit for British goods. His place was taken for a time by another colourful British traveller, Jonas Hanway, known also as the first gentleman in London to carry an umbrella for his own use.[13] But the situation could not be retrieved. Transit privileges were withdrawn by Russia, the factory at Resht was plundered, and Elton himself murdered 1751. What trade there was continued from the south.

At first there had been competition for this market between different British companies, the Courten Association, Merchant Venturers and New or English East India Company, but all of these were absorbed into the United East India Company in 1708. By the mid-1720s there were three factories in Persia, subordinate to Surat on the west coast of India, at Isfahan, Shiraz and Bandar Abbas. When they began, they faced opposition from Persian traders and obstruction at Court; later, they were in favour but often embarrassed by requests for naval assistance from the prince in power. After the Dutch and British had reduced the Portuguese influence in the area the Dutch, whose organization was government-sponsored, became the paramount European power. The French East India Company also operated from 1664 and further competition was provided by the Armenian merchant community.

Much of the British trade became centred on Bandar Abbas, in the Strait of Hormuz. The port was usually known as Gombroon, a corruption of the Turkish work for a Customs-house. Factories were maintained at Isfahan and Kirman, but Bandar Abbas was the only permanent establishment, until it was destroyed by the French in 1759. In 1763 the headquarters moved to the Basra Factory (Basra was in Turkish hands), but conditions continued to be difficult. When he was laying siege to the city in 1735, Nadir claimed that members of the Basra Factory assisted in its defence, while in 1743 the studied neutrality of the Resident led to him being imprisoned by the Turks for non-cooperation.

The archives of the former India Office are now part of the British Library. Specialists may consult this extraordinary treasure trove of books and documents relating to India and the relations of Britain with that sub-continent and the middle and far east. A vast card index records the interments in India of British soldiers, traders and administrators, their wives and their servants if imported, from the earliest days of contact. Countless biographies are interwoven on these cards as they review the victims of warfare, accident, disease and occasionally old age. Another extraordinary repository is the Factory Records of the British East India Company. At the time of writing these could still be examined in their original manuscripts, so that one could feel the paper and read the ink used to record the casual transactions, professional disputes and urgent intelligences of the Company's agents over two hundred years ago.

In 1729 the records for Gombroon consist of minutes of meetings, or Consultations, between a small group of people, usually including the Supervisor and Chief John Horne.[14] Little business being done, the notes are essentially diaries of current events, which have been put down in a rush of words with little punctuation. Notes covering the period when Daniel landed in December 1729, under the auspices of the Dutch East India Company, give a vivid impression of the alarming and changeable circumstances to which the residents at the Factory had to react.

On Friday 5th December they note that the local Governor has requested powder and weapons but they manage to put him off by explaining how short they are, how unsuitable their equipment and how much they wish to provide support against the Afghans. It seems there are, in fact, some cannons in a fort abandoned by the Afghans and they can spare a little powder. Confidential reports have indicated that Shah Thamasp is in possession of Isfahan so that outright refusal might be distinctly prejudicial. Shortly after, runners with letters from Mr Geekie in Isfahan tell them that Shah Ashraf has been beaten in two set battles by Shah Thamasp.

They congratulate the Resident and Mr Geekie on remaining safe and by the same runner write a congratulatory letter to Nadir Khan, assuring him of their readiness to serve His Majesty and magnifying the assistance they have given to those who supported him in Gombroon. This letter goes on to say how much the Honble. Company has suffered during the recent usurpation and asks humbly for his patronage because they are apprehensive that the Dutch might make claims against them with respect to a castle at Hormuz. Their case is that the Dutch endeavoured by bribes to corrupt the officers who kept the castle for the Shah, in an attempt to take it over. Out of sheer loyalty to his Majesty, however, E.I. Company officers interposed and occupied it. There was, of course, never any design to let the Afghans in and they propose to hand it back as soon as a suitable officer is appointed to establish control. The notes end with the pious expectation that this letter will obviate any ill impression that may have been made.

An important source of information on the actualities of life in Persia during the Eighteenth century comes from a book published in 1728 and in numerous later editions by Father Krusinski.[15] The later editions included passages by other hands, drawing on contemporary European knowledge of local affairs. On the name and title of Nadir, one of them has the following to say.

> The fame of Kouli Kan's exploits, the similitude which his name seemed to have with several names in Europe, and especially the great regard which he was observed to show the European Christians, gave rise to several rumours at the beginning of the year 1735, concerning the native country of this extraordinary man. They all tended to make him a Christian renegado; but the dispute was, who should have the honour of claiming him for their own. Ireland, for some

time, seemed to bid fairest; and we were formally told from thence, that he was born in that Kingdom, and that his real name was Thomas C'Allaghan, being descended from an ancient family so called. It was further pretended, that he had an eminent lawyer at Dublin his near relation, that he left Ireland when a child, and went to France where he became a monk, which gave occasion to a false report that he was of that Kingdom, and to strengthen all this was added, that he was known to be remarkably fond of Irishmen.

Whether all these circumstances were really believed by those who promulgated them, or were only a humorous imposition of some satirical wit, in order to ridicule the credulity of mankind, I will not determine. If the latter only, they were soon discredited again by the same means, there being a letter published in one of our daily papers, to the following effect.

From Rica at Paris to Ali-beg at Isfahan.

Dear Ali,
A ridiculous story is current in this country, which I would not mention to thee, if it had not credit with a great many people. 'Tis given out, that the glorious and invincible Thamasp Kouli, chief Khan and Vicar General of our Sublime Monarch, is an European by extraction, and born of Nazarene parents; not considering the absurdity and self-contradiction of the story; it being reported at the same time, that he is a Frenchman, a Fleming, an Englishman, a Scot, an Irishman, and I know not what besides.

If there is but a family in any part of Europe with a name

like Coulican (by which they murder the true name of our victorious Regent), and especially if of this family there is one vagabond strolling abroad, this is enough to make it immediately go down, that this Mr *Somebody*, who was thought to be lost, must be the famous conqueror of the Turks, the traitorous race of the unworthy Omar. But how impertinent is this? so that I may even blush while I am repeating it! Can the Nazarenes, who in other respects are so knowing, be ignorant that the term Khan, which they make to be part of the name of our great General, is only used to express a dignity very much like that of Marshal; only the Marshals have not, like our Khans, troops in their own pay? Are those Nazarenes ignorant, that, according to our religion, no foreigner, whether a proselyte or not, can be vested with all the authority and power of our sublime Sophi?

If the author of this letter had read the foregoing work, he would have found that Kouli was as much an assumed title as Khan, and that it signifies slave; and that even Thamasp was no more a proper name of this general than either of the others, but only the Prince whom he served: So that Thamasp Kouli Khan, taken together, means only the *Khan who is Slave of Sophi Thamasp.* This is confirmed by what has since happened, upon his taking on him the sovereignty, there being no more mention of either of these names in the title he now bears.

The supposed letter is a reference to the much more famous *Lettres persanes* of Montesquieu, first published in 1721, in which the selfsame Rica writes home to several correspondents about the curious habits and preoccupations of the French.[16]

At this remove the affairs of Persia must seem hopelessly confused to anyone not steeped in the history and traditions of the country. It would be very difficult to follow Daniel's exploits without some background information, but the same seems to have been the case for the intended 18th century audience. Part of the way through Daniel's narrative he creates an excuse to fill out a part of the book with a little general knowledge. "I am aware, my dear brother, that I have been speaking of the Afghans for some time.....". "I am now going to provide a brief account of the incredible history of these people, who for so long lived in profound obscurity." That may have been a literary device in use at the time. In one of Lady Mary Wortley Montagu's letters from Turkey, she writes, "Now I have mentioned the Armenians, perhaps it will be agreeable to tell you something of that nation, with which I am sure you are utterly unacquainted".[17] But in addition an uncomfortable coincidence starts to develop. A very considerable match is apparent between Daniel's account and that contained in later editions of Krusinski's work. When information about a particular place and period is assembled by different writers there are sure to be some close similarities. Each has to address the same major events, and particular anecdotes may have broad appeal. *The History of the Late Revolutions of Persia* provided insight into the life and affairs of the times. Originally by Fr Thadeusz Krusinski, it was subsequently edited by a Fr du Cerceau, who says that Krusinski was better placed than any other European to give a correct account of events. His memoir is augmented by less reliable reports from sundry newspapers. The second edition takes us to 1740 and covers the career of Kouli Khan after he assumed the title of Nadir Shah and including his conquests in India.

As to the reason Krusinski was so well-informed, du Cerceau gives it as follows. During the siege of Isfahan, no-one remained in the Jesuit monastery at Zulfa except the Procurator, who chose to protect the few movables the missionaries had left behind. Before the troubles one of his duties had been care of the riding animals, for which he built up a collection of animal salves and ointments and became skilled in their application. Word had it that he also treated human patients. After the fall of Zulfa the High Steward at Mahmud's Court, Efik Aghari, went down with an illness which his physicians found incurable. The Procurator was called in as a last resort, and being more farrier than physician he dosed his patient as he would an ass or mule. Success was immediate and his reputation increased. This enabled him to send for Father Krusinski, his fellow Procurator in Isfahan, whom he represented to be an even better physician. Father Krusinski visited Efik Aghari and after the expected salve and ointment treatment became one of his intimate friends. Efik was a close aide to Mir Mahmud, and the Father was thus able to gain a thorough knowledge of Afghan affairs.

Similarities between the Krusinski account and passages from Daniel's narrative are striking. Thus, we have Fr Krusinski:

> Calaate....the name they give to the rich vest with which the King presented the Governors of towns or provinces, as a mark of his satisfaction with their past administration and as a title which confirmed them in their post.

The Moginié version is:

> .....calaate. This is a brocaded coat of a kind which Persian kings give as presents or witnesses to their esteem, to those accorded an audience.

About the origin of the Afghans, Krusinski says:

> The Afghans, who were originally of the province of Szyrvan, which was anciently called great Albania, and which is situate between the Caspian Sea and Mount Caucasus, were

formerly subdued by Tamerlane, who could not reduce them till after many battles, wherein he cut a great part of them to pieces. But as this unmanageable people, not used to bear the yoke, were continually revolting, and took arms again upon the first occasion that offered, he thought he could not make sure of them, but by transplanting them to another soil.

In Moginié we have:

The Afghans originally lived in the Caucasus, from where they were removed to Persia by Tamerlane. Their nation was split into several branches between which religious differences fomented great animosity, kept under control when they were ruled by the Persians. The Afghan Abdalis were transposed to Khorasan, the Rasis or Shias to Hazerai, and the Sunni Afghans to Kandahar.

On the subject of prisoners, the Krusinski version is:

Their treatment of those who become their prisoners by the laws of war, has nothing in it of the barbarity we find among most of the other eastern nations. They look upon the selling of them into slavery to be a heinous inhumanity, which they hold in abhorrence. 'Tis true, indeed, that they keep them at home as slaves, and make them do the drudgery; but, besides that, in the time even of their slavery, they treat them with kindness and care; they never fail, if they do but please them, to restore them to liberty at the end of a certain term.

Moginié covers much the same ground:

The way they behave in victory would do credit to the best regulated society. Their prisoners are not enslaved. I have known many Georgian and Persian officers who have fallen into their hands and have been treated humanely. One, amongst others, was badly wounded and obliged to surrender to an Afghan, who at once asked if he could be exchanged for an Afghan prisoner. When the Georgian replied that he could not, the Afghan replied, "Well, stay with me for a year, do what you can for me and when that time is up I will send you home."

Krusinski is a little more anecdotal than Moginié with regard to the Afghans' method of fighting:

> As to their manner of fighting in a regular battle, they fall on thus: they place at first in the front of their army, in the nature of their forlorn hope, the best troops they have, which they call Nasackci and Pechluvan, i.e. Butchers and Wrestlers. These make the onset, and fall impetuously upon the enemy, without observing order or rank in their attack, but pushing forward in order to open the way for the rest of the army, which after this first shock, finds much less resistance. But when they are warmly engaged, those Nasackci retire in flank to the rear of the army, where they form a rear guard, which is only to force those whom they have engaged with the enemy to fight, and to hinder any body from falling back......As a soldier who was wounded there in his right arm only retired to have his wound dressed, a Nasackci came to him, and drove him back to his ranks, bidding him fight with his left hand, if he could not with his right; and adding by way of banter, that if he should also lose his left arm, he must bite the enemy with his teeth.

According to Moginié:

> Their troops were divided into two corps, apart from the cavalry, called the Nazachksis and the Pekelhuvans, meaning, more or less, the Butchers and the Athletes. The Butchers .... engaged the enemy first, creating a veritable turmoil.

Undeterred by the size of their losses because they could not make them out, they were unstoppable and opened a way for the Athletes who followed them. When they had achieved their aim they wheeled to the sides and filtered back to form a rear guard (it is necessary here to point out that in the East soldiers usually fight in a single line). There they prevented anyone from fleeing and forced them to return to the battle or killed them if they resisted. A wound to the arm was not sufficient cause to leave the battle, the wounded person simply changed his sword to the other hand and continued to fight until victory was won or he reached the end of his strength.

Krusinski also tells the story of Soleiman's lack of choice of successor and its consequences:

....Soleiman would not determine himself in this respect, and only said to the principal eunuchs that surrounded him,........that he left it to them, and the other grandees of the Kingdom, to consider which of his two sons, of whom he had an equal affection, was best for their purpose; that if they were for a martial king, that would always keep his foot in the stirrups, they ought to choose Mirza Abas; but that if they wished for a peaceable reign, and a pacific king, they ought to fix their eyes upon Hussain.

Thus did Schah Soleiman, through a folly and imprudence, of which he did not foresee the consequences, ... abandon the choice of his successor to persons who were interested to choose out of the two princes, not him that was most capable of governing the state, but him that was the fittest and most disposed to let them govern him.

In Moginié the equivalent passage includes:

The right of succession not being automatic in Persia, Soleiman was pressed to name his heir, but all he would do was to say that there would be no peace with Abbas and no progress with Hussain.

The lack of decision by Soleiman made the eunuchs all-powerful. Everything passed through their hands during his reign, and the principal appointments in the kingdom were filled by their candidates. Nobody disputed their right to choose the succession, and they chose the prince whose simplicity gave them the most influence.

At one point in his account Moginié says:
> If the Persians agree not to send an army against Kandahar it would be possible to make peace with them, at whatever price was necessary. But if the Court remains in its present drowsy state one could march strait to Isfahan and my successor could become king of Persia.

The Krusinski version is:
> If the Persians are obstinately bent to come and attack you, make your peace upon any terms; but if they sleep over this war, go and attack them even to the gates of Isfahan.

There are also some more general similarities. In Krusinski a carpenter from Courland called Jacoub uses cannon to attack the bridge at Shiras during a siege. Later, in his turn, Daniel rakes the bridge with cannon shot. Kandahar is said to have been fortified by European engineers during the time of Shah Jahan; Moginié does the same in the face of an attack by Nadir Shah. Daniel was present when Nadir concluded a peace treaty with the Turks. Krusinski gives the provisions of the treaty. He was also involved when Nadir is coaxed to become Shah by the acclaim of his assembled notables and army. The commentator in Krusinski (surely an Englishman) adds that both

Caesar and Cromwell tried the same stratagem but "had the mortification to see that neither the Romans nor the Britons were so complaisant as the slavish Orientals".

The Krusinski quotations come from an English translation, published in London in 1733. The Moginié account of 1754 is a briefer summary. Either the authors were strongly influenced by the same sources, or one inspired the other. Later in the Moginié narrative there is a passage on the Hindus. This section too looks like a plagiarism, possibly from another source.

☙ India, Persia and the west at the time of Nadir Shah

Daniel sets out on his journey as a brash youth. In Batavia he is naive and irritating but as the narrative develops in Asia the tone becomes progressively more sombre. The writer seems frustrated by his inability to influence events. The fortune he hoped for continually eludes him. The events in which he is caught up are of such unrelieved destructiveness and horror that the reader is left wondering whether any of it could be worthwhile. The passage from Bandar Abbas to Agra, with an extended interlude in Constantinople, takes only nine years, and at the end his health has deserted him. Soldiers, diplomats, treaties, invasions and rulers come and go. If one's finest efforts are likely to be overturned in a matter of months, why strive at all? After the excitement of the fighting with Nadir, weariness takes over and we feel our hero longs to stop, to die, as much as to see his brother. The parabola of Daniel's life is evoked by the famous coda to Matthew Arnold's *Sohrab and Rustem*. The majestic river floated on, out of the mist and hum of the low land, to waste itself in sterile plains before finally reaching the dark Aral sea. This passage is a poetic rendering of an evocative but more prosaic description by

Alexander Burnes of the region where the Moginié forebears supposedly flourished.

Even Sir Percy Sykes, soldier, orientalist, man of affairs and historian, seems to be exhausted and overcome in his 1915 *History of Persia,* by the senseless barbarity of the period. Nadir Shah, becoming increasingly cruel and erratic, was assassinated in his tent in 1747. Writing of his successors, Sykes says that the first was his nephew, known as Adil Shah, or The Just. He accepted responsibility for the murder of his uncle who "delighted in blood and, with unheard-of barbarity, made pyramids of heads of his own subjects", but later began to show the same qualities. After a short time he was dethroned and blinded by his brother Ibrahim, who in turn was murdered by his own troops. The next incumbent, Shah Rukh was an enlightened man, but one whose actions suggested that he was subverting the Shia doctrine. For this reason he was made prisoner and blinded by Mirza Said Mohamed, son of a leading doctor of the law. One of Shah Rukh's generals then defeated the rebel, blinded him and subsequently killed him and his two sons. The restored Shah did not last long, however. Two rebel chiefs seized and imprisoned him, blinded his general, fell out over who should wield power and the vanquished partner was added to "the long list of blind men".

In this world of the blind, tens of thousands are mobilised and thrown into pointless killing sprees in battle after battle. In such chaotic conditions, who produced the food? One may easily guess; half the population is unaccounted for. Women are mentioned only as labourers to build ramparts during sieges, as the Moghul's camp guard of lady toxophilists, or as occasional fickle figures in the background. After the spirited Mme. Kalb and her pretty daughter, from whose arms he was torn, Daniel rarely mentions women. He seems hardly to notice the loss of his wife in Isfahan. In India the Moghul's daughter makes more of an impact, but that is partly because she was a means to personal advancement. Village women, transplanted families and slaves must have kept the economy going and provided the resources and labour, necessary for the destructive regimes. In some ways, Daniel's faithful negro Abdala must have had a more adventurous time than he did himself, yet he hardly figures in the account, disappearing from sight then reappearing when required to perform some menial but essential duty. He is last heard of somewhere in India. It is perhaps indicative of his status that at one point Daniel hides his valuable goods with those which are least important, and these latter include Abdala.

Death and destruction, and heartless reaction to it, were by no means only an Asian prerogative. When travelling to Bengal some years later, William Hickey observed that the British and French navies, by that time fighting each other, had the crews on their boats replaced five times over, such was the attrition suffered through battle and disease. Russian campaigns against the Tartars and the Persians were extremely destructive. At the end of 1735 Russia under the Czarina Anne sent forty thousand troops to attack the Tartar Khan, but winter set in, nine thousand were lost to cold and sickness and the army retreated without even reaching the Crimea. After attacking Azov in 1736, Russian troops entered the Crimea and temporarily routed the Tartar Khan. Although Azov had fallen, the Russians were forced to withdraw by a combination of bad weather, disease and lack of supplies. Such ultimately pointless manoeuvres occurred in all theatres of war. They were continually cropping up in Europe. European rulers were quite as despotic and arbitrary as the Persian and Ottoman. Russia maintained an extravagant and bizarre court in a palace set in vast tracts of land reserved for hunting and peopled by foreign councillors, jesters, dancing bears and uncouth nobles. Outside, the country was completely undeveloped. There were few roads and no support system for the inhabitants. The Ministry of Health had 2 doctors and 1 physician on its payroll, but there was a standing army of 174,000 men, who mostly lived off the peasants. Since nothing was spent there were few outside loans and all returns from taxation could be lavished on the Court. By the end of the century the state of affairs in France was to bring down the monarchy. At the time with which we are concerned the French were interested in the War of Polish Succession because Louis XV felt it undignified to have a father-in-law who was a commoner. Instead of changing his wife, he saw a solution to this misfortune by putting her father, Stanislas Lesczynski, on a throne.

Of course, there was more to it than that. The Austrian Emperor and the Czar wanted a friendly ruler in Warsaw and chose Frederick, Prince of Saxony. France, on the other hand, wanted one who could vex the Habsburgs, which was also why she courted the Turks. In 1733 they elected Stanislas King of Poland, whereupon the Russian army advanced. Stanislas fled to Danzig, France declared war on the Emperor, Russia besieged Stanislas. Thus, short-term political advantage was coupled with overweening conceit to set in motion this extension of European diplomacy.

Through their emissaries in Constantinople the French tried to persuade the Turks to attack the Russians, but the Grand Vizier held out for a formal alliance. In Constantinople, the British and Dutch Ambassadors tried to frustrate French efforts. The Russians captured Danzig. France beat the Habsburgs, but in a sudden change of policy, supported Frederick and gave Lorraine to Stanislas instead. The defeat of Austria increased the security of the Ottoman Empire, allowing it to move against Russia and Persia. Events in Europe therefore had a direct bearing on the engagements in which Daniel was involved. His European counterparts had no more idea than he why they risked their lives in these bloody conflicts.

Events in India were as disturbed and confused as those of Persia.[18] Can we conclude that Daniel really had the positions he claimed? The Moghul Muhammad Shah died 26th April 1748 having ruled the Empire from 1719 until that date, except for a short interruption in 1720 and the appearance of Nadir Shah in 1739. The dynasty was started by Babur in 1526. The territory increased and its splendours multiplied under his successors, but the period of greatness was well over by the time of Muhammad. Being brought up in the Harem and ruling from the age of seventeen, he was not well equipped by training for the task he had to face. When young he was said to have been fond of both field sports and ladies. Latterly, a deep melancholy settled on him, and he preferred the society of religious teachers, with whom he discussed spiritual questions. The administration of the Empire was allowed to collapse. Courtiers, nobles and vassal Rajahs divided land and political power, and fought continuously for influence. Muhammad would assent to advice offered by his Vizier, but could never summon the courage to initiate effective policy. When the news was particularly bad the Emperor retired to his gardens to inspect newly planted trees, or went hunting on the plains. His Grand Vizier would also hunt or else move to a lakeside tent where he fished and admired the lotuses. No-one managed the affairs of state. This description, which comes from contemporary sources,[19] matches closely the impression given by Daniel.

In these circumstances the interests of the nobles drove them into factions according to their ethnic origins. The Court divided into two armed camps, the Turanis or Turks, and the Iranis who represented the Persian culture. Dissent at the centre spread through the Empire and combined with the secessionist tendencies of the Rajahs and inroads made by the warring Mahrattas who were gradually taking power at the periphery. The Vizier was a Turani emigrant from Samarcand, said to be drunken, indolent, harmless and kind, but presumably cunning and devious as well or he would not have survived. The leader of the Iranis after 1739 when he succeeded his father, was Safdar Jang, Subahdar of Oudh. He maintained twenty thousand of the best troops in the kingdom, paying them well, providing good equipment and looking after their creature comforts. Some of the best were Turkish speakers from Iran, called Kizilbashis in Persia or Moghuls in India, who were once part of Nadir Shah's army but elected to remain in India when he left. Their presence perpetuated the conflict between Shias and Sunnis in India.

Another feature of Indian warfare added to the confused picture.[20] In India princes were guided by their own Machiavelli, a writer named Kautiliya who lived at the time of Chandragupta, when the Greeks invaded the Punjab. He advised war only as an extension of statecraft. The first imperative was to trust no one and to make use of spying and subterfuge. The Prince should trick his ministers and allies, so as to test their loyalty, and the master of deception achieved his ends by avoiding war altogether. Should war be necessary, rules were provided for the organisation of the army and for engagement of the enemy. It was always better to avoid the risk of full scale conflict if this could be done by bribery or deception. To change sides unexpectedly might be more rewarding than to win but be savaged in the winning. Much had changed in the two millennia since Kautilya's treatise was written, and a new wave of invaders had brought their own traditions. Nevertheless, his teachings continued to have influence and would have made it exquisitely difficult for an outsider to appreciate a warrior who at one moment fought to the death with selfless courage, at another withdrew as if on a whim, and always deceived his allies as much as the enemy.

The combination of conditions prevailing at the time made defeat of Muhammad Shah by Nadir Shah almost inevitable. The latter entered Delhi and treated his captive well. He asked only for treasure, until a dispute in the city led to a massacre of its inhabitants. After that, the Persians rapidly decamped, leaving Muhammad and his dissenting nobles to try to restore the crumbling Empire. Nadir left Delhi at the beginning of May 1739, with all the goods his forces could carry. The historian Sir Jadunath Sarkar says that fifteen crores of rupees in cash were included besides jewellery, rich clothing and furniture worth 50 crores more (one crore is ten million rupees). Two famous and costly symbols of Imperial rule also went, the Koh-i-nur diamond and the Peacock Throne. Muhammad Shah held public audiences again, with exchanges of presents and conferments of rank. Coins were issued to replace those struck by Nadir. On the surface events returned to normal, but the army Chief of Staff and many of the powerful provincial governors had all perished, besides a host of well connected officers of lower rank. Ten to twelve thousand soldiers fell in a single battle and twenty thousand people were slaughtered in the sack of Delhi.

On the northern and southern boundaries of the Empire changes occurred which have a bearing on Daniel's account of his achievements. Nadir Shah captured the Punjab when he entered India in January 1739, defeating the Governor Zakariya Khan. On moving south he restored him to power, since he was evidently a good ruler. Zakariya Khan died on 1st July 1745 to the accompaniment of grief and lamentation and the heaping of flowers on his bier until the supply was exhausted. He left behind him three sons, who squabbled over the succession while the Emperor put off imposing his own will.

He rejected the Vizier's proposal to give two of the sons the provinces of Lahore and Multan, as likely to create a hereditary Turani dominion there. Many emigrants from Central Asia had settled in and around Lahore under the patronage of the last two viceroys and had built houses, tombs and gardens, rather as in Balkh or Bokhara. Eventually the Vizier obtained the governorship for himself, ignored the province and left it to a deputy to administer. The province sank into disorder until eventually in 1746 the Emperor agreed to appoint an effective deputy. Daniel claims to have become Governor of the Punjab and Lahore before 1742, while Zakariya was still exerting his just and powerful rule. It cannot be true, except perhaps as a reflection of the whim of a defeated ruler, piqued by the actions of his Persian enemy, wilfully bestowing an empty title on a foreigner in the security of his palace at Delhi.

Similar problems of timing and implausibility apply to the Deccan connection. The Mahrattas came to ascendency within the Mughal territory of north-western Deccan and the Western ghats. They started to gain power in the seventeenth century, and by the mid-eighteenth century had conquered great tracts of land across India to Bengal.[21] Theirs was an indigenous Indian movement based on tenets of military discipline and financed from the loot of successful warfare and payments by potentates who employed them in their own wars. Although they started as the people of the Maharashtra country of north central India, speaking the Maratha language, by this time their armies included many other nationalities or races, including Sikhs, Baluchis, Arabs and Portuguese. By the time of Muhammad Shah's downfall they were the significant force to the south of his territory. In the Deccan the titular head of state was the Rajah Shahu, a man who had ruled for several decades, while latterly power was in the hands of a dignitary called the Peshwa Baji Rao. In some accounts,

Shahu is said to have died in 1749, while one commentator, R.C. Majundar, states that he died sometime after 1739. Whatever the year, Raja Shahu had given the Peshwa a deed empowering him to manage the whole government on condition that he should perpetuate the Raja's name. The Peshwa decided to administer the kingdom on behalf of Ram Raja, Shahu's son by his second wife. His first wife opposed this decision and was offered the alternative of supporting the Peshwar or immolating herself in the sutee ritual. She chose the latter, and went to her doom with the traditional courage, the place where she died becoming holy ground. Ram Raja was put in prison in 1750 and died there in 1777.

Given these events, Daniel's account is highly unlikely; he died in 1749, before the widowing of the Rajah's wives according to most historical accounts. If the timing was in fact possible, his bride cannot have been the Rajah's first wife, and it is highly unlikely that the mother of the future puppet Rajah would have been allowed to leave for Agra. The best that can be said is that his wife could have been a subordinate consort, a sweetener for some political deal struck between Mughal and Rajah at some time during the latter's reign.

If the dates do not quite fit, the conditions of the time at least made it possible for outsiders to achieve recognition in high places. Laurence Lockhart, writing in 1926, translated from the Portuguese and commented upon an account of the times by a Frenchman called de Voulton, who was a private soldier in the Pondicherry garrison until he deserted in 1725.[22] An extract from the diary of someone working for the French general Dupleix in Pondicherry, indicates his career. Having won money at cards, he borrowed more, lost it and fled, abandoning his Dutch wife. After a number of adventures he contrived to be introduced to the Shah's vizier at Delhi, where he set up as a physician. When Nadir Shah invaded the country and plundered Delhi he enriched himself on his own account during the disturbances. At the same time he prevented Nadir Shah's soldiers from attacking the Vizier's house, so becoming both affluent and respected. In 1746, the chief physician to Nadir Shah was a man called Louis Bazin, so European physicians may not have been unusual. Later the historian Robert Orme, writing in a letter in 1755, states that, being in great favour with the Mogul, de Voulton was sent as Ambassador to the French together with a General and a large body of cavalry. Someone tried to poison the General but de Voulton continued with his mission. Orme regrets that the purpose of this embassy cannot be made out, largely because of the secretive way French affairs are managed by their representatives, who include a European renegade known as Abdullah Rumi Khan who first acted for them as an interpreter.

These two accounts provide us with descriptions of European adventurers with great knowledge of the country, who have benefited from self-taught skills and play a part in political affairs. There was no shortage of Europeans in Asia at the time. When escaping from Isfahan, Daniel found it effective to disguise himself in European clothes. The Portuguese and French were particularly broadly spread as advisors and supporters of the various powers.

De Voulton's story forms an interesting parallel to the account Daniel has left, or a suitable model, should the story be invented. Daniel is the type for a class of European adventurer, benefiting from a complex of interactions between east and west. History can be read as the interplay of individual actions and inexorable circumstances which determine human affairs. If the magical mixture which was Alexander the Great had not come into being, it is probably safe to say that the Greeks would never have reached Bactria and India. Eighteenth century figures such as the Afghan Mahmud and Nadir

Shah made conscious decisions to act as they did. Nadir Shah was effective, ambitious, intelligent and lucky, at least until he was assassinated. Like other great leaders, he had a marked effect on the political history of the region. Without him, history would have taken a different course, and his reputation lives to this day. But while the pattern of political unrest in which he was a player had much to do with the aspirations and folly of man, it was also driven by natural changes.

Persia is near the middle of the Fertile Crescent, a region of extraordinary developments in agriculture and civilization over the past seven thousand years. Many parts are now sandy desert. We tend to blame the deterioration on human exploitation, but the original fertile period coincided with a warm and damp phase of the earth's history. About five thousand years ago the climate became colder and, especially on its margins, the region was very sensitive to change. A warm phase commenced about 900 AD, lasting until 1300. The population increased, agricultural and pastoral areas expanded. From 1300 until the 19th century the climate again cooled. Each time conditions worsened there was a contraction of peoples from peripheral areas towards centres of cultivation. Central Asia was a semi-desert which bloomed in good conditions and quickly suffered in bad. Even when the climate was mild the tribes of the broad steppes were pastoral and nomadic, admirably equipped for rapid movement. Successive incursions into Persia to the south occurred when the steppe became desert. Pressures on agriculturists, brought about by shortage of food, led to internal unrest. The eruption of the Turks from Turan, which has so much to do with this narrative, was made necessary by the climate. Their nomadic life and martial traditions favoured them and they were able to manage conquered populations as if they were herds. Even the Ottoman word *raya*, originally used for subject peoples who had to pay taxes, implies that they were cattle. Alexander Burnes wondered at the size the invading hordes (a Turkish word) could attain. He concluded that their numbers were sometimes exaggerated by fear, but that any successful group picked up followers and swelled in size as it advanced to victory. At root, the nomads moved when they had to. The turmoil of Daniel's times was the product of changing physical conditions, acted out by the players with a nostalgic awareness of a richer past. The city of Merv became a symbol of this decline. Said to have been built by Alexander, it was capital of the once fertile land of Turkmenia, lying between Persia and Bokhara. It became great and prosperous in the tenth century under the Seljuks, forming a rich centre for the silk road trade and irrigated by a system of canals and dams which distributed the waters from its river. The Seljuks descended from the north and spread under Alp Aslan and his successors to form an empire to the south and west. After them came the Mongols and later the Uzbegs, until the Persians took the country from them in the sixteenth century. Visiting the region in the early nineteenth century, Alexander Burnes contrasted what he saw with its former state. "We shall be excused for dwelling upon the beauties of Merve, since we are still in Toorkmania, and impart an interest to its dreary solitudes, by describing this once beautiful oasis."[23]

❧ The role of Maubert de Gouvest

Besides the letter from Colonel du Perron and correspondence following from it, *l'Illustre Paisan* contains a dedication. Like similar passages in eighteenth century books in English, the style is formal and the intentions of the writer are not completely apparent. It runs roughly like this.

> To the Noble Lords
> the Chief Magistrate
> and the Great and Lesser
> Councils of State
> of the City and Republic of Berne

Noble Lords

The wise establishment, which gave to you the shadow of sovereignty, cast by the long arm of a real sovereignty that you must one day share, makes you a happy repository for the duties of your future state. You are, Noble Lords, the only body of young republicans in Europe, who would profess positively to value the talents of those of high birth. Could I trust to better hands than yours the story of an illustrious man, who by his own talents came near to a Throne, who by his gallant actions provided fitting support for the nobility of his ancestry?

I present this work to you, Noble Lords, and ask you to receive it as token of the high esteem and respect with which I have the honour to be,

> Noble Lords, your very humble and obedient
> servant, M. de G...

Who is M. de G.? Most commentators have concluded that the initials refer to the Chevalier Jean-Henri Maubert de Gouvest. The British Library catalogue describes *l'Illustre Paisan* as "Edited, or rather written, by M de G, i.e. J.H. Maubert de Gouvest." At one point in his magisterial book on Nadir Shah published in 1938, Lockhart writes,[24]

Before continuing on his way, Nadir dispatched a strong force to ravage the country between Peshawar and the Indus and to construct a bridge of boats over that river at Attock. On receiving word that this bridge was completed, he left Peshawar on the 25th Ramadan (6th January, 1739) and had reached the further bank of the Indus with all his forces by the 4th Shawwal (15th January).

A footnote says:

> Daniel Moginié (S[sic].H. Maubert de Gouvest), in his book *L'Illustre Paisan* (Lausanne, 1754), p.160, asserts that a French engineer named Bonal (who had, he says, joined Nadir at Tiflis in 1735) constructed this bridge. Moginié's work, however, is so highly imaginative in places that one hesitates to accept as correct any of his statements (such as this) which are not corroborated by other authorities. Sir Alexander Burnes, in his *Travels to Bokhara*, Vol.I, pp. 267-268, states that these floating bridges over the Indus could be completed in from three to six days; such bridges could only be thrown across the Indus from November to April.

Lockhart took note of his own reservations, and this is his only reference to Moginié or Maubert de Gouvest. The editor of the Cabédita edition, P-Y. Favez[25] agrees that the signature on the dedication suggests Maubert de Gouvest, but he points out that he was essentially interested in Europe while the author of the book shows a knowledge, not only of the east, but of the Pays de Vaud. He then indicates, and rejects, some other possible attributions. M. de G. was a figure as mysterious and intriguing in his own way as Daniel himself.

The nineteenth century French Biographie Universelle[26] includes Maubert de Gouvest, pointing out that he is less well known for his works than for his life, which was an adventure story in itself. He was born 1721 in Rouen, entered the Capuchin Order, but recognising that it was not his vocation, escaped from the Convent in 1745 and took refuge in Holland, with letters of recommendation for an Abbot who was French Consul at the Hague. He obtained a passport to Germany, volunteered in the Saxon army and participated with spirit and coolness in the battle of Dresden. He soon became an officer of artillery, but with the coming of peace, gave up the army to act as tutor to the son of his general, Count Rutowski. The knowledge he possessed of the interests and resources of different European countries gave him an entrée to government Ministries, but the freedom with which he passed on confidences led to his being denounced to the Elector of Saxony, King of Poland. He was arrested and incarcerated in the fortress of Koenigstein, where he remained until 20 May 1752. During his detention he was given books, pens, ink and paper and was able to write a range of speculative political works. Release came through the intervention of the papal Nuncio, but in return he had to become a monk again, and he set out for Rome to obtain a dispensation. When his hopes were dashed, he escaped from the Order a second time. After some months of difficulty he returned to France, went to Mâcon, then to Geneva and late in 1752 moved to Lausanne, where he lived on his wits and by intensive writing. To fit in with these new surroundings he became a Calvinist. In 1753 he published the *Testament politique du cardinal Alberoni*. As a result of its success he received further offers of work, and a short time after there appeared the first volumes of his *Histoire politique du siècle*. This contained passages which offended the French Ambassador. One account has it that in recompense Maubert agreed to act as the Ambassador's spy, another that he also quarrelled with theologians at Lausanne. At any rate, he moved again, and was in London at the end of 1755 where he received the patronage of Lord Bolingbroke.

While in London he came across a destitute man living on the streets with his wife and child. He offered to put them up in his lodgings, but after a few months the man disappeared. It turned out that he had gone to Holland, where he made some kind of a living using the name Maubert. The truth did not come out for a long time, and the true Maubert, now regarded as a spy, was shunned by his previous associates without knowing why he was suspect. Wearied by the mistrust, he left England and went to Rotterdam, arriving on the last day of 1757. It was only after a few months there that he came across the imposter. Although denounced to the magistrates, the false Maubert had time to escape to Hamburg, where he published frightful libels against his benefactor, which surfaced from time to time thereafter. Maubert offered his services to the Comte de Bruhl, Minister of Saxony, to help him in negotiations he was undertaking with Prussia. In doing so, he annoyed Frederick the Great so much that he was sent back to Holland. Next, Maubert looked for asylum in Brussels, where his writings so impressed the authorities that he received a small pension and was allowed to edit the Gazette and direct the royal printing house. As might by now be expected, his good fortune did not last. The fact that he was an apostate monk led him to leave, first for France and then back to Germany. For a time he was director of a troupe of French actors playing at Frankfurt during the festivities at the coronation of the Emperor. Arrested on 16 February 1764 as a vagabond he was thrown into gaol, where he remained for eleven months. A friend got him out and he left for Amsterdam where, two days after his arrival, he was again put in prison at the instigation of an aggrieved publisher from the Hague. He remained there two years, won the case brought against him by the publisher, and left for France. He died on the way at Altona in 1767, at the age of 46. Given the events of his life it is astonishing that Maubert found time to publish so much. Most of his writings were political tracts or recent history designed to support the point of view of one or other of his patrons, many were plagiarisms, but oddly, he also published a treatise on school education in France. The *Eloge* to Maubert in the *Nécrologie des hommes célèbres de France*, published in 1769, is a continual panegyric.

Some authors took a different view, which may, of course, have been based on the activities of his double. One wrote anonymously in 1759, while Maubert was still active as a writer, representing him as a spy and a fraud.[27] Another, F.-A. de Chévrier, published a *Life of Maubert* in London in 1761.[28] This ironical and libellous document, republished in 1763, evidently found a readership. De Chévrier explained his intentions in a Note:

> To spread abroad satyric libels is almost always a crime against society, committed by the misanthrope out of

envy or vengeance, who from one or other of these motives will attack even the most inoffensive member of the human race, but this is to give to the public a valuable service, to acquaint it with an unhappy malcontent from whom intrigues, knavery and impostures continually pour out: there is a need to unmask such people, especially when circumstances, and the murk with which these nonentities surround themselves, bring them to the attention of the police: awaiting the moment to act against them, those who by chance or experience have shed light on their doings must drop the veil and say, THESE ARE THE ENEMIES OF PUBLIC SECURITY!

According to Chévrier the events of Maubert's life were much as outlined above, but the gloss on his actions is different. In Lausanne the wife of a French doctor poisoned herself on his account. He was involved in a duel (or nearly so) with an Italian officer, and published a diatribe against a gentleman of Berne. His stay in Switzerland ended when the justiciary of Lausanne condemned him for his misdeeds to be chased publicly from town to the sound of a drum. Afterwards Maubert went to Germany, and, following the outbreak of war between England and France, to London to supply reports for several continental Courts. In London he was soon involved in a court action, held before blind Sir John Fielding, Henry's half-brother, a distinction he shared with Casanova and William Hickey.

All this seems to reflect a dispute far removed from our present preoccupations, yet there may be some connections.

Writing of censorship in France, Robert Darnton has pointed out that it naturally favoured publishing ventures in countries adjacent to that country, notably Switzerland and the Netherlands.[29] A variety of adventurous publishers, printers and writers produced works in French ranging from subversive fantasy and pornography to political attacks on the rich and powerful. The *libelle* was a means of undermining your enemy or opponent. It was often gossip dressed up as history, the writer representing himself as an editor or historian. The information might be provided as if by a spy, perhaps a Turk, an Englishman or a French speaker residing in London. The intention was sometimes quite gross, at others to work out a personal dispute, often to undermine some person or body in authority. In this case we have Maubert, whose character was at best compromised, involved in writing tracts on the borders of the French literary scene.

The choice of an eastern theme reflected contemporary interests. Lockhart states that the successes of Mahmud in 1723 resulted in his name and that of his father Mir Wais becoming well known in Europe. A book on Mir Wais entitled *The Persian Cromwell* was published in 1724 by an anonymous author "whose imaginative powers were far in excess of his zeal for accuracy". Another such was the *Mémoires de Schah Tamas II ... écrit par lui-même et adressés à son Fils* (Paris, 1758), which claims that Thamasp was actually the son of a Frenchman named Jolyot.[30]

The *Lettres persanes* of Montesquieu has already been mentioned. First published in 1721 this book was ostensibly the correspondence from Paris of a Persian called Rica to his friends and employees at home and from them to each other.

It dealt with the habits and extravagances of the Europeans and their religion, love, marriage and social institutions. Drawing on the writings of travellers such as Sir John Chardin for the eastern content, it was a vehicle for ridicule and open speculation under the guise of fiction. There were some antecedents and many successors. One of the latter was the *Lettres iroquoises* of 1752, published, it said on the title page, at "Irocopolis, chez les Vénérables". This was yet another production of M. de G.[31] The Iroquois visitor to Paris writes home to his friends about life and religion. The whole work was a lifting of the famous *Persian letters* even down to the phraseology: "France is the most powerful state of Europe" instead of "The king of France is the most powerful prince of Europe", and so forth. Later it was republished as the *Lettres chérakéennes,* ostensibly as a translation into French from the Italian by "J.J. Rufus, sauvage européen", a cheeky latinization of Jean Jacques Rousseau. It was said to originate from the College of the Propaganda in Rome (which took in natives of distant countries for training), but was actually published in Holland. Maubert had experience of writing false letters home from exotic locations. His enemy Chévrier was also at it. He published letters from a Siamese, a claimed translation from the Chinese and an Egyptian tale, "translated by a Genoese Rabbi". The structure and pattern of *l'Illustre Paisan* were commonplace at the time in works of complete fiction.

Daniel's narrative is distinctly episodic. This would not be surprising if written at intervals by an active and busy man, but could equally indicate that it has been cobbled together from different sources. The patchiness is most obvious with respect to dates (which for the most part agree with historical sources).

They are meticulously precise in some parts, down to the day, but absent elsewhere. Six dates are given between 23 December 1729 and 24 March 1730, there are five between 26 July and 23 September 1732. The period from 6 March to 9 July 1733, which describes a series of battles and skirmishes in the west, gets eleven dates. The deciding battle of the series and the accession of Nadir to the throne, in 1735-6, are less well dated. No dates at all articulate the hectic events in India. The transitions from one term to another to refer to Nadir, from Kouli Khan to Kausoli, to Shah, are also very abrupt.

Maubert was a rogue, an unprincipled political spy, if he was not an honest man misrepresented by some other rogue. Mercurial, skilled in subterfuge, active on the field of battle, and consorting with people of military and political account, he was well placed to dream up Daniel's story. All he had to do was add the exotic flavour, and there were many published sources on which to draw. Like Daniel, he was self-taught in military matters. He was a Protestant convert who escaped (twice) from a Catholic Order, Daniel a Protestant who thought of using monkish disguise. Clearly a rapid writer, Maubert knew the Swiss region concerned. He was familiar with the Netherlands and the Dutch, who provide inspiration for the first part of the book, and may have known enough of London to invent copy for its introductory pages. Errors of timing are the sort which would creep in if real events were described. Taken with the narrative, it is possible to see the dedication to *l'Illustre Paisan* as an ironic comment on those who represent the Republic of Berne, teasing them for their Whiggish beliefs. They see man as living by his talents, with a capacity to improve. In truth, deep forces stir the nobleman, revealing his character in the perpetual cycle of achievement and setback that are his aristocratic heritage.

❧ The origin of the Moginié parchment

The parchment in the wall was the source of Daniel's adventures. Without it he would probably have remained at home. The narrative tells us that in Persia he stopped thinking of himself as a peasant and took on the dignity of his ancestors as revealed by the genealogy. In India he used the original and a Persian translation - irreproachable testimony to lost grandeur - to support his plea when he wished to marry the Moghul's sister. How does this document stand up to scrutiny? Even in 1864 its veracity was being questioned. About the time of the *Chambers's Journal* version, S. Baring-Gould signed his name to two contributions to a similar publication called *Once a Week*, which take the story a little further.[32] The Reverend Sabine Baring-Gould, of Lew-Trenchard in north Devon, inherited a family estate and ended his days comfortably as Rector of the local church. He is remembered now as a collector of English folk songs. In addition, he was a prolific writer and tireless collector of anecdotes from his continental travels (*In Troubadour Land, The Deserts of Southern France*, etc.), of history and folk tales (*The Last and Hostile Gospels, Curious Myths of the Middle Ages*) and of a multi-volumed work on the lives of the saints. His interest in the Swiss story was typical.

Near Moudon, the ancient Minidunum, a small town on the high-road between Freiburg and Lausanne, in

the Canton de Vaud, lived, from time immemorial, a
family named Moginié, in the old tumble-down
Chateau of Chezales. At the time of which I am
writing, this family was represented by five brothers, the
eldest named Daniel, and the second, François. These
two are the subject of the singular story I am about to
narrate. .... The story will best be told by
extracts from letters written at the time, by a M.
Chollet, in London, to his father, the Commissary at
Moudon, which were printed in the *Journal helvétique.*

Two letters, which undoubtedly exist, are then reproduced in translation, and Baring-Gould goes on to comment on the supposed ancient origins of the family. From a letter, dated London, 22nd Nov., 1750, written to *M. le Commissaire Chollet, à Moudon,* by his son we get the following passage.

The two brothers left Switzerland at the ages of
seventeen and sixteen, and, two days before separating,
they each severally dreamt that there was a family
volume enclosed in the wall of the house. They went
together, in the morning, to the spot, with hammers,
and they found the book, which had been there 1000
years. By the writing of this book, of the last prince of
the family (notwithstanding that it was much decayed,
and that it is not right for poor people to possess titles),
it was found that the genealogy of Moginié commenced
with Armonigus, King of the Sacae, who was taken
prisoner by Cyrus, King of Persia, in the year 517 BC.
That battle was fought in the beginning of the reign of

Cyrus. The army of the King Armonigus, which consisted of 30,000 men, was partly cut to pieces, partly made prisoners; and there only escaped the prince Didon and Indus, the only son of the king, with a handful of men. These possessed themselves of Greater Georgia, of which they retained possession for many centuries.

Baring-Gould then continues the story.

I can give a few additional details, however, though they throw little or no light on the puzzling question which continually recurs to one's thoughts: Was François Moginié the subject of a hoax, or the originator of one?

The account given by him of the discovery of the volume is evidently pure invention. His story was, that both he and his brother dreamed on the same night that an important MS. was hidden in the wall of their house. On the following morning both brothers met at the same spot with picks in their hands..... Du Perron's story was, that Daniel had the book examined in the East, and had been informed that it contained a complete genealogy from Armonigus, King of the Sacae, to a descendent who migrated to Europe, and who, having eloped with a Roman lady of distinction, was obliged to live in retirement, a love-in-a-cottage sort of life, in Switzerland. ....

In constructing this "cock-and-bull" story, it is possible that François may have got hold of Ctesias; though it is strange that he should have done so, as he was by no means an educated man; and besides, if he did, it is remarkable that he did not make his story harmonise better with the account of the historian. Herodotus and Xenophon make no mention of any king Armonigus, nor of a war with the Sacae; but Ctesias speaks of a king *Amorges*. Curiously enough, no one seems to have remembered the passage of the historian till long after François had left, and Moginié himself never alluded to it.

The second part of Baring-Gould's account in *Once a Week* continues the story. Although he does not say so, he was now in possession of a copy of *l'Illustre Paisan* which furnished information for further speculation.

> I confess that I am somewhat perplexed about the story of the MS. genealogy. That Daniel actually discovered an old record in the wall of his house is not improbable. I have a copy of one before me now which was found in a similar manner in a Norfolk mansion; and it is possible that he may have persuaded himself that it contained the pedigree of his family, a persuasion which was deepened by the foolish remark of an ignorant Swiss pastor. But I must give Daniel's story of the discovery in his own words, for I own to being quite unable to say where the truth ends and fiction begins. The memoirs are addressed to François in the form of a letter.
>
> ".....Do you remember, my dear brother, that evening which we spent with our father at Uncle D'Oron's,

together with our cousins, Villars-Mendras, Jean Dutoit, and our godfather Baptiste? It was an odd meeting, and I remember it distinctly now. One of our cousins, de Villars, who had been thrashed by a nobleman of the neighbourhood for hunting on his property, was lamenting bitterly the difference in rank which rendered it impossible for him to obtain satisfaction from this gentleman; and he recalled bygone times, when the family of Moginié was as famous in the country for its opulence as for its antiquity....... Jean Dutoit, who had formerly studied for the ministry, and who was a natural wag, chaffed us a good deal about our nobility, which, said he, was so venerable that it was quite out at the elbows. He predicted that we should one day find the title-deeds of our lordships in some nook of the house, like as did the sons of our Moudon neighbour; and that we should in the same way discover that we were fourth in descent from some royal house, or else that, as in the case of Monsieur N-, it would be ascertained that some infanta of Portugal had strayed up the Rhone to Seyssel, and had come ashore at Nion, to be our great-grandmother."

A west Asian origin for the Moginiés sounds improbable, but stranger fluctuations in fortune have occurred to other families. Every pedigree is unique and infinitely unlikely. Is it probable that Marie-Josèphe-Rose de Tascher de la Pagerie and Aimée du Buc de Rivery, two girls from Martinique, should have ended up respectively as Empress Josephine of France and

Sultan Valide to Mahmud the Second? In Josephine's case, at least, there is no doubt. Perhaps some infanta did stray up the Rhone. Baring-Gould thinks a passage has been lifted from Ctesias. He was a contemporary of Xenophon and private physician to Artaxerxes Mnemon, whom he accompanied in his war against his brother Cyrus in 401 BC. He wrote a history of Persia, and also one on India, the remaining fragments of which would have been better known in the eighteenth and nineteenth centuries than they now are. Since his accounts did not always agree with those of Herodotus and Xenophon, there was a tendency to dismiss him as a serious historian. According to Chambers's Encyclopaedia of the time, "Ctesias compiled his history from oriental sources, and it is not wonderful that his statements often contradict those of Herodotus." *The Cambridge History of Iran*, a more modern source, observes that the world described, peopled by eunuch chamberlains and femmes fatales and featuring poisoning, exquisite tortures and vicious harem intrigue, gives some reflection of the royal court, but that on balance it should be disregarded.[33] Later information which uses Ctesias as a source therefore also has to be reappraised. Being on the spot, however, Ctesias could be more reliable than Greek historians writing from the perspective of the Greek world. We are accustomed to accept the familiar view. If the Siebenbürger Saxons had not had printing presses and hated their landlords, Vlad Dracula would now be just a courageous defender of the Christian faith. Young Turks are called Attila by doting and sentimental parents. The study of history also fills the past with numberless alternative worlds, interpreted in ways which we, from time to time, desire. Another consideration comes from the dates supposedly given on the parchment. In the 1754 version the first relevant passage reads

> In 928, the Bojacides who descended via secondary kings of the Parthians from Darius, son of Hystaspes, formed a party and dethroned the Calif, whose place was taken by one of them called Amarxes. His posterity reigned until 1062. Then the barbarians, who are not otherwise identified, overwhelmed Persia.

The second reads,

> This book is written by hand, it is dated 1069 AD, the sixth since the fall of the Bojacid empire, one thousand six hundred and seventeen years since the battle against Cyrus.

That provides a date of 548 BC for the battle against Cyrus (not 517 BC, as in Baring-Gould), and the Amorgines family are said to be Saces, or Soghdians, who lived in the vicinity of Samarcand or Bokhara and spoke an Iranian language. Cyrus was indeed waging war, having conquered the Medes in 550 BC and was about to obtain the submission of the Hyrcanians and Parthians in 549 BC.

Of course, the second date could not possibly come from Ctesias, so that if not authentic the story must have another source. The Caliphate, originally centred on Baghdad eventually became divided into several parties. One of these, the Samanid Dynasty, originated near Samarcand or in Khorasan. They were probably Sasanian, and their territory included Khorasan and Soghdia. In 928 part of their land south of the Caspian Sea was seized by the founder of the Ziyarid Dynasty which ruled until 1042. The date and place, if not the name, are just about right. Suitable candidates as barbarians are the Karakhanid Turks, who are known to have established themselves in former Samanid territory. More generally, the Oghuz Turk confederacy was at this time emerging from Turkestan, displaced as a result of conquest and unrest in the northern and western Chinese territories. They were in the process of forming an extensive Islamic empire in Persia, Mesopotamia and Asia Minor, the Ziyarids ending as their vassals.[34]

Such migrations as the Moginiés were supposed to have undergone were not uncommon. From the earliest times warriors and clerics were among the most mobile sections of society. The seventh archbishop of Canterbury was a Byzantine from Tarsus who had studied in Syria, and many similar examples are found during the first millennium of the Church. The Seljuk warrior Alp Arslan, who flourished between 1063 and 1072, defeated the army of the Byzantine Emperor Diogenes Romanus. The Emperor's forces included a body of mercenary French and Normans, commanded by Ursel of Baliol, a kinsman of the kings of Scotland.[35] Perhaps Daniel's parchment is confirmation, rather than theft.

Pierre-Yves Favez has a more prosaic suggestion.[36] He has established that the Moginié family lived in the Vaud for many generations before the events which are noticed here. The surname, he says, is a descriptive one, recalling the occupation of guardian of "modzons" or heifers, in patois "modzeni". This is known in a number of variants: Moginier, Mojonnier,

Mogeonnier, Moiougny, Moionny, Mogeniz, Mojonis, etc. There are records of the name at Chesalles-sur-Moudon in the second quarter of the 16th century. Local documents reveal a Pierre Mojonnier, sometimes called Pinget, and his wife Perusson living there modestly between 1536 and 1550, in a house on a parcel of land which had restricted use, for they were forbidden to plough it. The subsequent history of the family can be traced from this point.[37] With this interpretation the family ancestors have dwindled from kings to cowherds.

ᛦ The English connection

François Moginier was the second of ten children born to Jacques Antoine Moginier and Madeleine Moser at Chesalles. His elder brother Daniel was baptised on the 31st August 1710. He became godfather to his cousin Maria Magdalena Moser in the German-speaking parish of Moudon on 31st December 1727, two months before his presumed departure to the Netherlands and the east. François was baptised on 16 March 1712. Four years elapsed before the birth of the next child. On 2nd October 1729 at Chesalles François became godfather to his brother Jean-Jaques, the fifth child of the family, born in 1720. There is a record of his marriage to Elizabeth Kemp of Mansfield, Nottingham at St Anne, Soho, London (in which he is recorded as Francis Moginnie), on 25 January, 1742. Children were born to the couple two years later and a year after that, but each time they died young. On 30 March 1746 a son John was christened at St Anne, Soho, their only child to survive infancy. Other children were born in 1749 (Lewis, christened at St Martin-in-the-Fields) and Daniel in 1751 .

Those are the facts. Further English records of Moginies can be traced to François through his son John, except for two. One was Jacob, a widower, whose second marriage took place on 3 September 1783 at St Marylebone to Martha Walter "of the same parish spinster". There was also Mary Moginie, a widow, who married Richard Wright in 1782 at Saint Luke, Old Street, Finsbury.[38] We can only speculate on their relationship, but two other members of the Chesalles family were Abraham Jacob, born 1716 and Jacob, born 1725. Church records contain others with similar names; for example a Daniel Henry Moginot was christened at St Anne, Soho in 1742; his name does not stray very far from the range of spellings used by known relatives.

Moginie is a sufficiently curious name for the question of these relationships to have come up before. Extracts from an unpublished manuscript written about 1880[39] show that the position of Jacob has never been quite established, and also that the profession of Protestant faith was an ongoing preoccupation. John George Moginié, the son born in 1746, was said to be an accountant with a French business house in Lime Street, London. He had twelve children, five of whom survived infancy. When his wife died they were sent to a boarding school and were never subsequently told anything of their family background. John himself retired on an annuity to devote himself to preaching the way of salvation through a crucified Saviour. The manuscript also records a Jacob Moginié who lived in Swallow Street, London, believed to have been uncle to Francis and surviving until 1800. There had been a chapel in the same street, where Huguenots and other refugees from "Papal tyranny" gathered to meet and worship.

Jacob is said to have been part of the congregation, although in fact it was closed before his time and moved to premises in Soho.

Other references to François come from *l'Illustre Paisan*, from the note published in *The Gentleman's Magazine* in 1750, and from the letters of M. Chollet to his father published in the *Journal helvétique* in 1751. From these we can reconstruct the following picture. Sometime between March and June 1728 he was in the Netherlands with his brother, where he became engaged in service to an Englishman, Mr Dillington. He and his employer were still on the continent when the christening took place in 1729, unless he returned for the occasion, but by 1750 he was running a public house or tavern in London (the French word is *cabaret*). He read Col. du Perron's notice in a London paper on 18 October of that year, and by May 1751 was in Moudon. There he obtained copies of baptismal certificates for himself and his brother, duly authorised by seals of the bailiff and of the Republic of Berne. Thus equipped, he set out for India with the Colonel to collect Daniel's legacy. In June 1751, a letter arrived at Moudon stating that he and the Colonel were in Venice. About the same time a letter to London from Corfu said that he hoped to be in Constantinople by the end of July.

After that, we have only the account in *l'Illustre Paisan*. Following the dedication, there is a short section entitled *Avis essentiel au lecteur*, which outlines the details. The colonel seems to go to some lengths to convince Francis of the richness of his inheritance, saying that there is no doubt that the Emperor will pay up. He provides him with Daniel's gold watch (the other, set with diamonds, was too valuable to risk on voyage), a decoration in the form of a gold lion weighing an ounce and a half and a topaz seal mounted in gold bearing the arms first seen on the parchment genealogy. While Francis was away, his wife and two children were provided for by Mr Tomlinson, a merchant living in King William Street in the City. The last reference to Francis is in a letter to Tomlinson from a Mr Gogham in India, dated 26 October 1753. Gogham is described as *directeur du comptoir anglais de Surate*, interpreted by Baring-Gould as "agent of E.I. Company at Surat". His letter provides an altogether less flattering account of the colonel than we have so far been led to expect.

> As you requested, Sir, I have had the Swiss adventurer in whom you are interested followed to the Court in Agra. I have also gathered some information on General Daniel Moginié, whom you know as prince Didon & Indus. Through the illness of your client, who is strongly incommoded with dysentery, I have been favoured with his presence in my house for eleven days. I am not the least surprised, Sir, that you doubt the existence of the fortune which he has come so far to seek. The manner in which Capt. du Perron announced it to him was enough to make the most credulous suspect him, and one would have to be more generous even than you are to advance money against promises so badly expressed. Capt. du Perron's story is a proper muddle. The title of Prince which he has given to General Moginié is completely unknown here, where there are only princes of Moghul blood and sovereign Rajahs. His titles of Generalissimo and

> Chamberlain are equally imaginary. The Emperor is waited upon in the interior of the palace by women and eunuchs, and there is no other Generalissimo of his armies but himself. The powerful Rajahs whose forces form more than half the Moghul army, would not take their orders from a soldier of fortune. Up to the death of Shah Jahan they would not even serve the Moghul, except as auxiliaries. Their forces are the equal of those of the most powerful Electors of Germany; and their nobility, as scrupulously preserved, renders them quite as punctilious. They only obey the Emperor in person.

Gogham then goes over the supposed details of Daniel's career in the east, pointing out further mistakes by du Perron. The princess Daniel married was called Neidone-Begum, but the colonel renders this as a title - Didon and Indus. The colonel suggests there is a will, without realizing that in law the inheritance may be disposed of by the Emperor as he chooses. Francis must await an audience, in the first place with the Nabob in whose house he is lodging in Agra. The letter goes on,

> On the day of his audience with the Nabob, that dignitary will give him an extensive work written in French, which Daniel Moginié left with him to give to the brother. The brother arranged that if five years after news of his death was published in Europe François Moginié had not appeared, the manuscript was to be sent to the French ambassador in

Constantinople, so that it might be passed via the Swiss representative to the family living in the Pays de Vaud.

This work is no other than the autobiography of the Omrah. As I intimated that I was eager to learn how this illustrious man had arrived at such a high position, M. François Moginié has taken the trouble to copy the manuscript himself, and has sent me this copy in a sandalwood box decorated in silver-gilt and worth at least a hundred and fifty rupees, with a letter a copy of which I enclose herewith. I also enclose a copy of a second which he wrote to me, in which he permits me to publish the autobiography. I believe that such a book should be completely authentic, and should therefore be put in the hands of a Swiss publisher, so that under the eyes, as it were, of those who know the family, it will have the stamp of truth and not be confounded with mere romances. It will also have to be polished a little by a more literary hand. Truth is embellished by a pleasing style. However, I would recommend that the editor retains the naive style; the Omrah commits some grammatical infelicities. He was a very spirited person, and people who knew him well have assured me that few of the nobles in Agra expressed themselves better than he in Persian, the language of the Court and Palace.

I have the honour to be, etc.

There follows a letter from Francis to Mr Gogham.

Agra, 17 July, 1753

Monsieur,
Since I have been in this great city I have seen many things which merited my attention, but there is nothing which could make me lose sight of my debt to you for the help you have had the goodness to provide since my arrival in Surat. I felt that I could not better show my appreciation than by sending the account which my brother left of his adventures. I have now managed to transcribe it, having set to work before reading it completely myself. There are many things in it I do not understand, and no doubt I have made some quid pro quos. But you are cleverer than I, and can correct my mistakes. One would have to know this country well to understand it all. My brother Daniel thought me cleverer than I am. I ask you, Monsieur, in your spare time to put things right. It would comfort me to be able to make this known in my own country, where my relatives and friends have made fun of my brother and myself, when I told them what I learned from M. du Perron. I wish also that good and generous Mr Tomlinson could see a summary of it. Mr Robert, his eldest son, who has always been very kind to my wife, will perhaps read it to her and my two sons. It would interest them greatly. It is important that they should know what is better or worse about this place compared to London. I kiss my hand, if it pleases you,

to Madame Gogham and pretty Mistress Nanci. I hope to send them something to show that I think of them.

I am, etc.

Another letter from the same to the same, 9 September.

The casket is nothing, Monsieur, and does not deserve your thanks. I wish the Lord Nabob, who sent it to me with a present of betel, had supplied one in solid gold - I would have sent you that. I count you a sincere friend. In truth I need one because here I find myself like a man dropped from the clouds, despite M. du Perron's lessons. The Emperor is unwell, and I with him, but impatient to know what the future holds, because after all, time hangs heavy on those who wait. The Nabob tells me to keep up my spirits and remain hopeful. I am so sorry we have no language in common, so that we can converse. Instead of the troop of walking statues with which he has stocked my rooms, I wish he could just give me the money which they use up - I would send it to my wife and children. That would convince them, if I should call them here, that they come to a well-lined nest. ...

Like Gombroon, the East India Company left detailed records for the trading station at Surat, on the Indian west coast north of Bombay. The base was subordinate to Bombay, and the entries in the reports consist of accounts and letters between

Surat and the directors at Bombay. Some passages from the time of Francis's supposed visit give a flavour of the exchanges and the personnel involved. The volume for 1751 starts on Wed. 7th August, and constituted the diary of James Henry Lambe, Chief for Affairs in Surat and subordinate to the Honble Richard Bourchier Esq., President of the Coast of India, Persia & Arabia, Governor established at the Castle of Bombay.

Many Company representatives are involved in the business. Present at Surat were Lambe, Francis Pym, Richard Hunt, Titus Scott and William Delagarde. Letters from Bombay to Surat are addressed to "Honourable Sir and Sirs" and signed "affectionately" by Bourchier. A letter from Bombay Castle at this time, signed Rd. Bourchier, was also signed by George Scott, I. Sewell, Thomas Lane, Cha. Crommelin.

A long section in October describes a disturbance or civil war. This ends with the Council apparently leaving the factory at Surat after agreeing to a disadvantageous peace treaty with the local Mahratta powers. "Article of Peace proposed to Haffis Masood Caun 1 Oct. 1751" signed by Lambe and others. This results in a most important loss of status for the Factory. William Mackenzie then writes to Bourchier from Surat objecting that, as Military Council he has not sufficient rank nor resources, nor good enough officers, to carry out the defensive tasks required. In a letter to Lambe, Bourchier withdraws him and his Council and replaces them by Henry Savage and Laurence Sulivan, with "country powers" to restore the Company's position at Surat. This letter is simply addressed "Sir", as relations between the two stations deteriorate. Sulivan is evidently an effective manager and negotiator. Lambe disappears from the documents, while Sulivan goes on to become a prominent member of the Company and a Director in London. In March 1751 a peace was agreed, and Bourchier writes to say that he is pleased the conditions are more favourable to the Company than could reasonably have been expected.

The records for 1752 to 1754 are mostly financial accounts, letters etc. There is comment on the state of the market at Mocha, where piece goods are sold and coffee taken on for shipment to England. A dispute develops between Bombay and Surat concerning the quality of chintz. Bombay complains that the cloth arrives with imperfections. The respondent in Surat says this is due to the practice of beating it after it has been dyed and washed, and that he cannot examine every yard of every bale. Bombay replies that every servant of the Company must ensure the best possible quality, and if those immediately responsible have not the time, then the Director himself should do the job. On a less irritable note, the Dutch Company's Director comes one day to take his leave before proceeding to Batavia.

A person who does not appear, however, is Mr Gogham. If he existed, he was not an important member of the Surat establishment and not the Company Accountant. However, there seemed to be a sufficient number of military men of uncertain quality and agents in outlying stations, for him to have been there without being noticed by the official records. The port of Surat was called Souali. Francis actually mentions it, rather than Surat itself, in his letter to Gogham, who was perhaps established there with his wife and his daughter Nancy. Francis concludes his letter of 9 September, 1753, with these words.

> Since you are sure that my brother's writings would make a book, let it be done soon. But pray give me your word that it will not be a romance. What we have needs no polishing by writers of fiction. If it should contain any errors I would give the lie to them by sending from here a true version of the original in my possession. One more thing I ask of you, that you put at the head that M. le commissaire Chollet and his son, with Mr Tomlinson and his, are those to whom I dedicate the edition.
>
> I am, etc.,
François Moginié

The book came out, but neither of these names appear in a dedication. Colonel du Perron, or Captain, as Mr Gogham calls him once and *sieur* du Perron in another place, was not much valued as an observer of Indian affairs by that supposed servant of the Company. He is not much help either in establishing credentials for the story. Baring-Gould believed in his existence, saying that he belonged to a respectable French family that settled in Berlin, and that while in Europe he recruited craftsman on behalf of the Moghul Emperor. He also refers to him as a clever rogue. Dredging the records for notable characters of the time, we find in the French National Biography one Abraham-Hyacinthe Anquetil-Duperron. He was born in Paris in 1731 and, becoming interested in oriental languages at an early age, he determined to procure manuscripts of the Zoroastrian sacred books.[40] He engaged as a soldier in 1754 in order to get to India. There he left his military position and spent an eventful year or two, at one time undertaking a difficult journey across country to Pondicherry to escape the consequences of the war between England and France. On meeting his brother, also arrived in India from France, they travelled up the west coast to Surat. Mere coincidence, no doubt; this could not have been the man, but what of his brother? At least, the anecdote shows that it was common for adventurous and curious Europeans to enlist as a means of travelling to the east.

As to Daniel, records of his baptism exist, and of his younger brother's marriage and children in London. The notice of du Perron's advertisement in 1750 and the Chollet letters published in the *Journal helvétique* in 1751 both appeared before the book. They could have been inventions, by Francis or Chollet or both. If so, then one or other may have been responsible for all the incidents and may have written the book. At present, however, we have no reason to doubt the authenticity of these documents. If they are true records then Daniel must have gone to India. And in that event, the style of *l'Illustre Paisan*, the place of publication, mixed content, and the fact that his name is on it, all point to Maubert as the author who embroidered the bare facts of his life.

It has been suggested in Switzerland that the colonel needed Francis with him to release the inheritance. After that, Francis was murdered or perhaps accidentally died; we last glimpse him suffering from dysentery. Even if so, it was hardly necessary for Daniel to leave a memoir. All the details of his adventures are reflected in contemporary writings, with which Maubert was extremely familiar. He had an outline available in the Chollet letters. He was familiar with Switzerland and the Netherlands. He could also draw on his own experience of warfare, supported by false credentials, and of rapid changes in fortune. Parts of the book are plagiarised, and we know he was adept at pirating published works. The story of the parchment could well be a fabrication. If so, it was prepared by someone before 1750 since it makes its appearance in the advertisement. The account of the lineage is rich in historical detail, and could only have been invented by someone with a knowledge of history from the time of Darius to the tenth century. It is useful in providing motivation for our hero's actions and a passport to noble marriage. Such information would be available to Maubert, who had access to several libraries.[41] The book was published in a republic but could be read as a parable showing the importance of breeding.[42] M. de G., the political essayist, was used to writing to such an agenda. Somewhere there must be a tiny crystal of fact which, when added to the mixture, will precipitate the definitive account of these events. Until that is found, the uncertainty remains.

NOTES AND REFERENCES

1. Lady Mary Wortley Montagu (1763) *Turkish Embassy letters*. Pickering, London, 1993, with an introduction by Anita Desai.
2. Moginié, Daniel 1754 *L'ILLUSTRE PAISAN OU MEMOIRES ET AVANTURES DE DANIEL MOGINIÉ, Natif au Village de Chézales, au Canton de Berne, Baillage de Moudon, mort, à Agra, le 22. de Mai 1749. agé de 39 ans; Omrah de la I^e Classe, Commandant de la Seconde Garde Mogole, grand Portier du Palais de l'Empereur, & Gouveneur du Palngëab, Où se trouvent plusiers Particularités Anecdotes des derniéres Révolutions de la Perse & de l'Indostan, & du Règne de Thamas-Kouli-Kan. Ecrit & adressé par lui même à son Frère François, son Légataire.* Pierre A. Verney, Lausanne. Another edition, Lausanne, 1761, "AU DEPENS DE LA COMPAGNIE", has on the title page, "Publiés par Mr. Maubert." Also London, 1754, Frankfurt, 1755. German translation, Berne 1755.
3. *l'Illustre Paysan. Daniel Moginié de Chezalles. Récit de ses aventures.* 1912 Reprint of 1754 edition. Sack, Lausanne. *L'extraordinaire odysée de l'illustre paysan Daniel Moginié Général du Grand Mogol.* 1988 Reprint, with preface by Micha Grin and foreword by P-Y. Favez. Cabédita, Morges.
4. Anon. 1864 The romance of a Swiss boy. *Chambers's Journal of Popular Literature, Science and Arts.* Fourth series, No. 51, 803-807, December 17, 1864.
5. It should really be *L'illustre paysan*, but since archaic spelling is used in the title it has been retained throughout when referring to the book. *The illustrious peasant* does not work in English; he is a renowned rustic, a natural nobleman. The

name Moginie is used with or without the accent in different sources.

6. The London Journals & Newspapers consulted were: *The General Advertiser* Daily, Oct.18, 1750; *The General Evening Post* Thurs Oct.18-20, 1750; *The Gentleman's Magazine* October 1750; *The London Evening Post* Oct.18-20, 1750; *The London Gazette* Tues. Oct.16-20, 1750; *Old England, By Argus Centoculi, Inspector-General of Great-Britain* Sat. Oct.20, 1750; *The Penny London Post or The Morning Advertiser* Oct.17-19, 1750; *The Rambler* No. 60, Oct 13 1750; *Read's Weekly Journal or British Gazetteer* Oct 20, 1750; *The Whitehall Evening-Post or, London Intelligencer* Oct.18-20, 1750.

7. In the *Journal helvétique*, October and December 1751.

8. Bruijn, J.R., Gaastra, F.S. & Schöffer, I. 1979 *Dutch-Asiatic shipping in the 17th and 18th Centuries.* Nijhoff, The Hague.

9. Guthrie, William 1777 *Geographical, Historical, and Commercial Grammar and present State of the several Kingdoms of the World.* Knox, London. Other sources consulted are: Rickleffs, M.C. 1993 *A history of modern Indonesia since c.1300.* Macmillan, London; Schmidt, J. 1996 Dutch merchants in 18th-century Ankara. *Anatolica*, 22, 237-260; Vlekke, B.H.M. 1959 *Nusantara. A history of Indonesia.* Van Hoeve, The Hague.

10. Huguenot Library, University College London.

11. See, for example: Cassels, Lavender. 1966 *The Struggle for the Ottoman Empire 1717-1740.* Murray, London; Lockhart, L. 1938 *Nadir Shah.* Luzac, London; Markham, C.R. 1874 *A general sketch of the history of Persia.* Longman, London; Morgan, D. 1997 *Medieval Persia 1040-1797.*

Longman, London; Sutherland, Lucy S. 1952 *The East India Company in eighteenth century politics.* Clarendon, Oxford; Sykes, P. 1915 *A History of Persia.* Macmillan, London. Two Vols. The most detailed account of the period, and most informative on its sources, is Lockhart, L. 1958 *The fall of the Safavi dynasty and the Afghan occupation of Persia.* CUP, Cambridge. Brief studies of the principal players in Persia and Afghanistan are found in Anon. 1945 *Persia.* UK Naval Intelligence Division; Dupree, L. 1973 *Afghanistan.* Princeton UP, Princeton, New Jersey.

12. Burnes, Sir Alexander. 1834 *Travels into Bokhara, together with a Narrative of a Voyage on the Indus.* 3 Vols. Murray, London.

13. Taylor, J.S. 1985 Jonas Hanway: founder of the Marine Society. Scolar Press, London.

14. The British Library: Rare, Oriental and India Office collections.

15. Krusinski, J.T. (Judasz Tadeusz) 1733 *The history of the late revolutions of Persia: taken from the memoirs of Father Krusinski, Procurator of the Jesuits at Ispahan; who lived twenty years in that country, was employed by the Bishop of Ispahan, in his negotiations at the Persian Court, for the Emperor and King of France; and was familiarly conversant with the greatest men of all parties. Done into English, from the original, lately publish'd with the Royal Licence at Paris, by Father du Cerceau, who has prefixed a map of Persia, and a short history of the Sophies; with curious remarks on the accounts given by Tavernier, Sir John Chardin, and other writers that have treated particularly of that government and country &c.* J. Pemberton, at the Golden Buck in Fleet Street, London.

Another edition: *To which is added an appendix, giving an authentic account of the dethroning of Sophi Thamas, by his general Thamas Kouli Kan; the advancement of that General to Imperial dignity, and his many victories over the Turks and Moguls, down to the present year 1740.* J. Osborne, London 1740. Reprinted as: *The history of the late revolutions of Persia.* Arno Press, New York. 1973.
Translation of: *Histoire de la dernière révolution de Perse,* Briasson, Rue Saint Jacques, à la Science. Avec Approbation & Privilege du Roy. 1728. Another edition: 1729. Reprinted as: *Histoire de Thamas Kouli-Kan, nouveau roi de Perse, ou Histoire de la dernière révolution de Perse, arrivée en 1732,* Briasson, Paris. 1742, 1743, and as *Histoire des révolutions de Perse depuis le commencement de ce siècle jusqu'à la fin du règne de l'usurpateur Aszraff.* 1742. Jean Antoine du Cerceau lived 1670-1730. Author of appendix not stated.

16. Green, F.C. 1925 Montesquieu the novelist and some imitations of the "Lettres persanes". *Modern Language Review* 20, 432-442.

17. Mary Wortley Montagu *Turkish embassy letters.*

18. See, for example: Burgess, J. 1972 *The Chronology of Indian history.* Cosmo Publications, Delhi (first published 1912); Haig, W. & Burn, R. (ed.) 1937 *The Cambridge history of India. Vol. IV. The Mughul Period.*Cambridge University Press, Cambridge; Keene, H.G. 1972 (reprinted) *The Turks in India.* Idarah-i Adabiyat-i Delli, Delhi; Majumdar, R.C. (ed.) 1977 *The history and culture of the Indian people. The Maratha supremacy.* Bharatiya Vidya Bhavan, Bombay; Orme, Robert. 1763-78 *A history of the Military transactions of the British Nation in Indostan.* London; Sarkar, Sir Jadunath 1964 *Fall of the Mughal*

empire. Vol.1. 1739-1754. Orient Longman, Bombay.
19. Sarkar, Sir Jadunath 1964 *Fall of the Mughal empire. Vol.1. 1739-1754.* Orient Longman, Bombay.
20. Mason, P. 1974 *A matter of honour: an account of the Indian army its officers and its men.* Jonathan Cape, London.
21. Majumdar, R.C. (ed.) 1977 *The history and culture of the Indian people. The Maratha supremacy.* Bharatiya Vidya Bhavan, Bombay.
22. Lockhart, L. 1926 De Voulton's Noticia. *Bulletin of the School of Oriental Studies, London,* 4, 223-245.
23. Burnes, Sir Alexander. 1834 *Travels into Bokhara, together with a Narrative of a Voyage on the Indus.* 3 Vols. Murray, London.
24. Lockhart, L. 1938 *Nadir Shah.* In Lockhart's 1958 book he writes of *l'Illustre Paisan* and a few other titles "Some of the books that I consulted, I was able to discard almost immediately." Later he uses the word meretricious.
25. Favez, Pierre-Yves, 1988 Foreword to 1988 Cabédita edition of *L'Illustre Paysan,* pp. XIII-XXIII
26. Michaud, J.F. 1843-65 *Biographie Universelle, Ancienne et Moderne.* Desplaces, Paris.
27. Anon. 1759 *l'Espion, ou l'histoire du faux Baron de Maubert. Auteur de plusieurs libelles qui ont paru pendant cette guerre. Pour lequelles il a été exilé de la Hollande.* Liege, Aux depens de l'auteur.
28. Chévrier, F.A. 1763 *Histoire de la Vie de H. Maubert, soi-disant Chevalier de Gouvest, gazettier a Bruxelles, et auteur de plusieurs Libelles Publiques. Mise en lumiere pour l'utilité Publique.* A Londres, chez les Libraires Associés.
29. Darnton, R. 1995 *The forbidden best-sellers of pre-revolutionary France.* Norton, New York.

30. These references are from Lockhart's *Fall of the Safavi dynasty*.
31. Balmas, E. 1962 *Les lettres Iroquoises de J-H. Maubert de Gouvest*. A.G. Nizet, Paris. (Reprint of 1752 edition with introduction).
32. Baring-Gould, S. 1864 The brothers Moginié. *Once a week*. Parts I & II. 10, 345-349, 371-376, March.
33. Yarshater, E. (ed.) 1983 *The Cambridge History of Iran. Vol. 3. The Seleucid, Parthian and Sasanian Periods.* Cambridge University Press, Cambridge.
34. Frye, R.N. 1975 *The Cambridge History of Iran. Vol. 4. The Period from the Arab Invasion to the Saljuqs.* Cambridge University Press, Cambridge; Gershevitch, I. (ed.) 1985 *The Cambridge History of Iran. Vol. 2. The Median and Achaemenian Periods.* Cambridge University Press, Cambridge.
35. Sykes, P. 1915 *A History of Persia*. Macmillan, London. Two Vols.
36. Favez, Pierre-Yves, 1988 Foreword to 1988 Cabédita edition of *L'Illustre Paysan*, pp. XIII-XXIII
37. For valuable information on the Moginie family: Janet Bulkeley, notes and discussions; Moginier, Louis 1935 *Généalogie de la famille Moginier de Chesalles s/Moudon, de 1620 au 31 décembre 1935.* Recherches effectuées aux archives cantonales, à Lausanne, en juin 1935, par Louis Moginier, fils d'Ernest, Lausanne. Provided, with later additions, by Dr Henri Moginier, 1991; International Genealogical Index of The Church of Jesus Christ of Latter-day Saints.
38. London, Faculty Office, 15 August 1782.
39. Burrell, E. M. ca.1880 *Summary of the history of the Moginie family with genealogy traced down to the present date*

from our English ancestor Francis Moginie born 1712. Arranged for William J. Moginié by his 2nd cousin E.M. Burrell, Broadstairs, Kent, England. Typescript provided by Peter Moginie, 1991.

40. Which he succeeded in doing. The collection was deposited in the Paris library and he published *Zend Avesta, the work of Zoroaster, translated into French*, 1771. See Markham, 1874, *History of Persia.*

41. He also published *Memoires militaires sur les anciens. Ou idée precise de tout ce que les anciens ont écrit relativement a l'art militaire.* Utrecht, Spruyt, 1762 This work includes references to Xenophon. It also lists *Illustre (l') Paysan* (sic) 1761 as a work "by the same author". For anyone with a more respectable reputation that should clinch the matter.

42. Another of his enterprises was *Conversations on polite life. Exemplified and illustrated with eastern and other stories tending to form in the minds of youth, sentiments becoming that station of life, which gentlemen are educated to adorn.* London, Lockyer Davis, 1755. This was a translation of *Ecole du gentilhomme, ou Entretiens de feu Mr. Le Chevalier de B***.* Verney, Lausanne, 1754

THE MEMOIR OF DANIEL MOGINIÉ

PART I

Daniel addresses his brother, telling him how he leaves Switzerland to travel to the Netherlands Indies with his Dutch patron, M. Kalb. The older man dies on the voyage, Daniel reaches Batavia and M. Kalb's family, eventually to be abducted and removed as a result of jealousy over his love for the daughter. A vagabond strolling abroad, he goes to Persia during a civil war, joins the Afghan side and helps to defend Shiraz against the Persians. The position of the Afghans becomes untenable, and he changes sides to throw in his lot with the Persian military leader Kouli Khan.

In the midst of plenty I have never felt perfectly content. Whether from vanity or tenderness, I have always hoped to seem rich and strong in the eyes of my close family and to share my wealth with them. Whilst struggling against misfortune, I wished only that they could know my successes. When I became infinitely better off than I ever dared hope, this desire turned into a passion. I do not fully understand these impetuous feelings; perhaps I am simply motivated by the tender and sincere love I have for my brother François. Certainly I cannot remember without emotion the bond that caused us to seek our fortunes in such different ways, and I have always feared that when I became rich my dear brother might still be groaning under the burden of indigence. Such is the legacy inherited from our forebears over many centuries. To assuage these feelings I continually sought news of you. For eight years there has been scarcely an English, Dutch or French boat at Surat that I have not approached with enquiries. I have written to Madras, Bombay, Pondicherry, Gombroon and Isfahan, but never received a satisfactory response. Captain Durant of Marseilles promised two years ago to enquire in the Pays de Vaud or contact the French ambassador in Switzerland. As I am sure noone acting on my behalf has been negligent, I am reduced now to fearing that my dear brother is dead, or that he lives in a state of obscurity which renders him quite untraceable.

Being struck down by an illness which allows me no more than a few months of languishing life, I consecrate my last hours of leisure to you, my dear brother, if you are still alive, to present this my life story. By that means you shall know how divine providence has favoured me. Undoubtedly some aspects of the story of my advancement in the Court of the Moghul Emperor must read like a fable, but this little memento, if it reaches you, will present to you a brother you would otherwise have lost. I have obtained from my sovereign and liege master, the Emperor, a promise that he will treat you and your family with the good will he accords to me. My plan to lure you to this happy country will not end with my life. I leave friends who will seek you. If their efforts are rewarded, the gift of these papers will be the first witness of my love. Would that your fortune in Europe were great enough for you to turn down mine. But if you are not perfectly settled, put aside the timidity of our compatriots and come here. Your true country is the one where you are best provided, and I dare to hope that this will be it. The word of the Emperor is inviolable. He has given me his word that if you come, you will receive all my possessions. Profit from my labours and receive a fortune which would have made me the happiest of men, had I been able to enjoy it alone.

Daniel now reminds François of their dream, the discovery of the manuscript in the wall of their house and the search for a linguist who could translate it. He then recounts the story of his life after they parted.

Monsieur Kalb gave me back the book, with a sheet of paper on which he had written down a resume of the account he had read to me. I asked him for it so that I could pass it on to you. I was very keen to contact you, and excusing myself for not staying longer I asked him if he would please wait till the following day for an account of the present state of our family. You and I then had a little disagreement about the document I got from M. Kalb, which you wanted to show your new employer, in the hope of impressing him. We sulked for the rest of the day, and in the end you left it with me without even taking a copy. The following morning, when I asked you to come with me to see M. Kalb, you said you proposed leaving immediately on a boat to Utrecht to rejoin your new master. Irritated by your tone I left abruptly and went alone once more to M. Kalb's house, where I found him waiting to offer me a meal on my arrival. We discussed the family. He was very sympathetic when he heard the way our parents and relatives lived, and urged me to give up soldiering at once, since there was no future in that direction. "So long as you are poor in the land of your fathers", he said, "your genealogy will seem no more than a fable. Although you know it to be true that will not do much good. You cannot make your fortune in Europe; follow my advice instead. I was poorer than you at your age, and if I had stayed here I would now be as poor as my father, who had nothing. Thirty years ago I signed up as a simple sailor with the East India Company. I worked my way until after 20 years I had risen so far there was no more to wish for. Unlike me, you have a friend to help you on your way. Come with me to Batavia. I am setting out again in a month or six weeks. I will look after you on the journey, and if you prove yourself worthy I will continue to support you when we get there."

I pointed out that I had signed on for two years military service, and had received more than two hundred ecus in uniform and salary which I would have to give back before I could dare ask for a discharge. "Don't worry about that" replied the generous M. Kalb, "give me your word and I will finance you." When he saw me hesitate he went into his office and came back with forty ducats which he made me take. "Go back to Bois-le-Duc", he said. "I am sure Captain Stürler will do what you ask. I knew a General of that name in The Hague, who is a very fine man, and no doubt your captain has the same qualities." I also pointed out that I had no knowledge of the Dutch language. "Well", he said, "didn't you tell me your father made you learn German? In that case, it will only be three months before you speak Dutch as well as me."

I took the forty ducats from M. Kalb, without giving him a definite answer. I wished to discuss the matter with you, my dear brother. Imagine how I felt when they told me at the inn that you had left for Utrecht. I ran to the canal to catch the next boat. Having got to Utrecht, which seemed the most likely place to look for you, I went to the Anvers, where your employer was staying. We were reunited there, ashamed of the way we had parted. When I told you what M. Kalb had suggested you urged me to seize this opportunity to restore the family fortunes. I pressed you to come and share the risks and rewards, but you wanted a quieter life. You offered to lend me everything you could for a year, and this witness to our affection touched me to such an extent that, taking you in my arms, I repeated the pact we had made at Chesalles. After our last meal together you accompanied me for a league of my journey. I embraced you and left, my dear brother, feeling we would never meet again in this life.

In Bois-le-Duc things turned out to be easier than expected. As generous as M. Kalb, the Captain refused my offer to buy myself out. "If you are going to seek your fortune in the Indies", he said, "you will need all the funds you can get. I will loan you all you say you owe me, and when you are as rich as your patron you can pay me back. Only return the uniform you got from the Regiment. I wish you all the best and God be with you."

The 24th of June 1728 had been fixed as the departure date for the fleet. My patron took me with him when he loaded some luggage at Texel, and introduced me to the Captain as a young German gentleman who would travel as far as Batavia. My trunk and bed were delivered in my name, and my board was paid in advance. Perhaps my good benefactor had a premonition of the mishap that occurred on the journey.

The winds did not allow us to set sail until the 27th of June. Once moving we quickly made up time, and by the twelfth day of our voyage we were at Madeira. As we crossed the equator M. Kalb was lively and introduced me to the ridiculous baptism which is almost a religious rite among seafaring men. By the time we approached the Cape of Good Hope, however, he had become very ill. The surgeon declined to bleed him, thinking that after landfall the beneficial air would be sufficient to effect a cure. A violent storm kept us sixty leagues from shore for two days, and the illness worsened. High fever and delirious fits reduced the patient to extremity. In a lucid moment this generous man decided to help me support the loss if he should die. He wrote a letter in the form of a will for me to take to his wife. He recommended me as a relative whom he had asked to accompany him, and bequeathed me his sword and watch, along with the clothes in his wardrobe trunk and a hundred ducats in coin. He suggested that if I proved myself to be a man of courage and probity their daughter might be a good match for me. When he made these last provisions he was already sinking fast. In vain did we hope for the benefits of landfall; he died while Table Mountain was still on the horizon.

My distress was beyond description. Although an unsentimental character, the Captain too was touched and comforted me in my despair. I only came to my senses when the preparations for the funeral were discussed. They wanted to bury him in the cemetery at the fort. I was opposed to that, and spent the best part of a hundred ducats having the body embalmed in a lead coffin. The Captain refused to receive it, and when I asked the pilot to do so he unashamedly demanded another dozen ducats to lodge it in a corner of his cabin. To relieve my anger at this pettiness I went off to visit the colony, which is some eight or ten leagues inland from the fort. It is almost entirely populated by French people expelled from their country after the revocation of the Edict of Nantes. Nowhere in Europe can they live in more comfort and prosperity than at the Cape. The five days I passed became almost a holiday, and I was told that life was always like that. The lands are worked by slaves bought from the Company or by Hottentots who will work for a week for a handful of tobacco. I drank the most wonderful wine and ate all manner of game and wildfowl. I also met a countryman of ours who had made an annual income of five thousand florins over fourteen years. He was called Turretaz and came from Orbe, not far from our home town. He had been manager to one of the Company directors at Batavia and was so honest in that capacity that when his master died he did all he could to find the heirs to his fortune. Through them he obtained a commission to buy wine and livestock at the Cape to ship to Batavia on behalf of the Company, and in five years amassed a five thousand florin profit. Becoming disenchanted with this job he sought some land and became a settler. The Company sold him eighteen slaves for two thousand florins and provided ten others on credit. He borrowed during the first year so as to get good stock for sowing; and the Lord blessed his efforts to the extent that by the end of the year he had paid off his creditors, bought the loaned slaves and had enough left to invest in a good herd of cattle. Each year his plantation grew, and feeling settled, he arranged for an orphan to come out from Amsterdam to marry him. By the time I was there she had given him four sons and a daughter. I have never met a more honest, contented and successful person. He told me his story and I outlined mine, whereupon he invited me to remain with him. I felt that my duty to my late patron was now owed to his wife and daughter. Wise and honest Turretaz, while commending my sentiments, pointed out some of the difficulties and dangers I might face if I went, which my lack of experience prevented me from seeing. But I would not be swayed. I had no doubt of the goodwill the widow of my benefactor would bestow on me.

During the first three months in Batavia I could only

congratulate myself on my choice. Respecting her husband's wishes, Mme Kalb welcomed me as a valued relative. She appeared to accept the idea of adoption he had put to her in his letter. Seeing that her daughter was not averse to me she engineered situations where we could be together and accepted the fact of our love. She seemed to take pleasure in encouraging our feelings, and not doubting that she approved, we looked forward to our union while only regretting that it might distance us from her.

At this time I decided to make myself thoroughly acquainted with my patron's business. I mastered the art of arithmetic, which he had started to teach me on the boat. I then took daily lessons from an instructor, or Dominie, as he was known, who was travelling through, and my knowledge of German enabled me to perfect my Dutch. I made an effort to associate myself with the principal figures in the colony. Soon there was no great house where I was not welcomed and the General himself honoured me with his interest and the promise of the first suitable vacancy which became available. I believed I was in a position to ask Mme. Kalb to make public her approval of my marriage to her daughter. She promised to do so after the six months of her mourning, and I was so confidant of her support and my position in the family that I went without the least concern to Malacca to sort out some business the family had with Company Factors there. After about a month correspondence from Mme. Kalb ceased. Worried by this turn of events I decided to wind up affairs in Malacca, but new business, which she initiated, kept me away for another month. Just as it was finished the Commandant made me an officer in the Company garrison, with orders to remain at my post. To leave, he insisted, would be a capital offence.

Imagine the despair this brought to someone in love. I had in my possession a considerable sum of money which had been owed to my patron. It allowed me to bribe a Chinaman from Batavia, who was there with his junk. At the risk of all future gain I set sail with him and arrived in Batavia, where, disguised as a Chinese and unrecognised in the street, I made my way to the house of Mme. Kalb. The first person I met there was my love. Our joy at being reunited blinded me to the danger I was in. As we walked in the garden she told me of the plot which had been brewing since my departure. It appeared that the only son of one of the Batavia Councillors had expressed his intentions towards her, and her mother was happy to give her support. "I am afraid" added Mlle Kalb, "that what I suspected is true, my mother will never accept you as a son-in-law. Your absence allowed her to submerge her first positive feelings for you. Simple friendship would not explain the uneasiness with which she has awaited your return. She likes you, I am sure, and I think the commission you got from the General in Malacca was contrived by her and my new suitor to keep you away."

Mlle. Kalb was a spirited seventeen-year-old full of vigour and enterprise. She was accustomed to get what she wanted from her mother. Always wilful, she was used to independence, which made her rail against the obstacles erected to the only true passion she had ever felt. We loved each other equally and resolved to do everything to remain together. So fearless was she that she never flinched from the proposal that we should flee together to Europe. Mme. Kalb came upon us in the midst of our discussion. Perhaps she overheard these last remarks. At any rate, this lady whose restrained manner I had always admired, was beside herself with rage. Her daughter, who had never before received anything but tender love, now experienced her transports of fury. After being berated and struck she retired to her room, and I was left with her mother, my emotions divided between resentment at her attitude and knowledge of what I owed her. In her fury she was deaf to any appeal. Instead of the deluge of scorn and reproaches which I expected, however, I was now faced with tears and obstinate silence. I felt I had to speak, and did so with the respect owing to the widow of my benefactor but resolutely reminding her of the encouragement she had given to my hopes. With many expressions of sadness, Mme. Kalb then commenced to explain the situation. She told me the Trustees of her family fortune disapproved of my proposed marriage, and she had been obliged to go along with their wishes because they controlled her daughter's future wealth and income. What use are riches, I cried, if she is to be unhappy? But my appeals and threats did nothing to change her mind. She left me as angry as she had come.

As I was walking alone pondering the crisis I was in, my rival came into the garden accompanied by his father and many notables of the Colony. I made to hide, but it was too late. One of them promptly left the party, calling on the others to keep an eye on me. I went up to them and addressed them politely, receiving an equally gracious response. This was just to keep me occupied until their friend returned, for they knew he had gone to inform the General of my presence. Half an hour later a detachment of the guard appeared and their officer arrested me. I was taken to the Fort, thrown into a cell and passed the night on a miserable pile of straw which had served as a prisoner's bed for more than a year. I was eight long days in that hole, never seeing the light of day and fed on a handful of rice and a crock of water twice a day. On the ninth day they brought me before a tribunal like a common criminal, manacled hand and foot. The fresh air and blinding light caused me to swoon but stirred no pity in my captors. They dragged me to the door of the room where they cast me to the ground like a corpse. I do not know what remedies they used to bring me to my senses, but when I came to I found myself lying on a wretched bed in a dungeon. My shoulders were deeply scarred and the wounds had been rubbed with salt and vinegar. After eight more days I was taken again before the assembled Council. Seeing that I was not able to support myself on my knees, the General ordered a wooden block to be brought, on which I could sit.

My sufferings over fifteen days, both in body and spirit were such that I no longer cared to defend myself or excuse my disobedience, for which the official punishment was death. But when I heard them accuse me of ingratitude and seduction, of imposture and intended incest, when I heard them impugning the memory of my benefactor and calling me his bastard, I came to my senses with a will to deny these atrocious accusations. Honour, and the memory of love, made me eloquent, and the truth of my words had such force that the General and his Council, silenced in their astonishment and vexation, could say nothing in reply. I noticed several of the Councillors wiping their eyes. The General ordered me to be taken to the Fort infirmary, and as I left I heard him say, "It would be an injustice".

Someone put me into a decent bed where exhaustion and a little soup had their effect, and I fell into a profound sleep. The principal accusations against me were ingratitude and seduction, compounded by injury to the name of my patron when it was claimed that I was a product of his misspent youth. This being so, I told them the whole of my story from my departure from Chesalles to my flight from Malacca. The General had been born no richer than me and owed his fortune to a patron who had recognised and valued his ability. He could therefore sympathise and, as an honest man, had been moved by my gratitude to M. Kalb and the discretion with which I had spoken of his widow and of the relations between his daughter and me. He had no wish for these matters to be pursued. "He is innocent of the charges brought against him," he told the tribunal, "and if this goes further we should blush to have treated him so badly. Leave family matters to the family. As to the formal misdemeanour, that I must follow up. I believe it may be pardoned since he did not agree to enter military service. However, to ensure that this behaviour does not spread I propose to send him back to Europe on the first available boat with whatever M. Kalb bequeathed to him."

This judgement was only countered by a man as honest as himself, called M. Master, who was both rich and childless. He persuaded the General not to pronounce a sentence which would still, in effect, dishonour me, but to allow me to be treated as he proposed. This worthy gentleman visited me soon after I awoke the following day. He sat at my bedside, where he exclaimed, raising his hands towards the sky. "Generous is the lord who grants one's prayers!" I took him for a Minister, who had come to strengthen my courage in the face of death, and I therefore replied that I was a servant of the Lord, who had given me the strength to accept my fate. He smiled and explained my mistake.

"You no longer need to be resigned, my dear boy," he said, "Your troubles are over. It is I who must accept my fate, that I have not been blessed with a son like you, who would bring me joy and satisfaction in my old age. What sadness it is to me that I have no heir who would cherish my name after my death and carry it proudly himself. Think no more of the troubles which have assailed you. You will find other young ladies as agreeable as the daughter of your first patron, who would be glad to link their futures with yours."

 I interrupted my consoler to say that I loved Mlle. Kalb with all my heart, that she was my betrothed and that before God as before men, I wished for no other but her. "What are you saying?" replied M. Master, "I must tell you, and you must accept, a secret which puts paid to those hopes. Mlle. Kalb, having been told that you are her natural brother, has accepted the hand of your rival. You will get nothing but anguish from believing there was more than fine words between you. With the help of the doctors you will get your strength back. Leave Batavia for a while; I promise you will not regret the new circumstances brought about by the envy and slander of your enemies. I only ask you to see in me a second M. Kalb. Honour me with the respect you had for that gentleman, and I will treat you with no less affection than he did. You have in me a friend, a benefactor, a father, even more able than he to take care of you."

 M. Master consoled me with a truly paternal tenderness in my anguish over the fickle Mlle. Kalb. He left me only when he saw I was entirely resigned to losing her. The following day I received from Mme. Kalb a letter and a present of sweetmeats and liqueurs. Despite what she told her daughter about me, I have no doubt that she was sincere in her protestations of good faith with respect to the accusations she had made against me. The Captain of the boat on which I had come from Europe started her suspicions when speaking of me as a German gentleman, as M. Kalb had made me out to be. She was confirmed in her belief when M. Kalb referred to me as a relative. In the end, I accepted the innocence of the widow in this respect and replied, reminding her of her promise to repair the damage she had wrought. It was no more than a day since I had received the visit from M. Master. Before I was completely restored he had already proposed a plan wherein he would adopt me and make me his heir, while I should take the lead in making an honest fortune. But my new patron revealed this plan to a false friend who passed it on to some people who hoped to be his beneficiaries. That led me into a second persecution, less violent but better organised than the first. One evening he asked me to dine with him so as to inform his relatives of the adoption, and tell them that next day I was to leave for China, where he proposed I should trade. Before I could get to him I was seized in my room in the infirmary by four negro slaves, who quickly gagged me and bound my hands and feet. In that state they put me into a tightly curtained litter which they raised onto their shoulders, and I felt myself being carried with great speed through the streets. At the quay I could hear my captors putting my equipage onto a long-boat, and had no doubt they had orders to throw me into the sea. I now had time to reflect on this turn of events, and my first thought was that the abduction could not have been carried out without the knowledge of the General. That calmed me for the moment, since I did not believe that his actions could be completely evil. My captors arranged my litter in the centre of the boat. They spoke only to organize the rowing, giving me no clue as to my fate. Soon they hailed a vessel in the lines and clambered aboard it. I was hoisted to the deck in my litter and taken to a stateroom, where the Captain from the boat on which I went to Malacca extracted me from my cage. The sight of him boded no good. I believed him to be my enemy, and he noticed my alarm.

"Believe me", he said, "I have no plan but to take you away from Batavia. You leave behind persons who love and esteem you. Swear to me that you will never come back and I shall show you that I am among their number." I gave my oath and the captain embraced me. "Go", he said, "and make your fortune elsewhere. You are too good for these parts, where you disturb the tranquillity of all the hopeful relatives of rich old men and all the favourites of rich widows. The General has engineered your departure to protect you from the fate you would have suffered sooner or later at the hands of M. Master's relatives. I am myself not unaware that you could be a dangerous rival for the hand of Mlle. Kalb. But neither the relatives nor I would wish you any ill far from Batavia. On the contrary, they asked me to give you, when you swore to leave, this bag containing three hundred piastres, and I hereby add another hundred, which I urge you to accept. The General returns to you the hundred ducats that the late M. Kalb bequeathed you. Here are the two trunks with your clothes, which he retrieved from Mme. Kalb, and a gold chain with his arms on it, which he presents to you. And that is not all. Your cousin gives you this diamond, which she asks you to wear for love and as a mark of the friendship and esteem in which she will hold you for the rest of her life. Give me receipts for these various articles when we set foot at Malacca, where you must remain at the Castle until the fleet leaves in two months or thereabouts. Let us drown the memories of your adversities in a few bottles of this good Cape wine."

I was treated as an officer by the Commandant of Malacca, whose friendship made my detention pass agreeably, and as it turned out, usefully. He was a French refugee who had been for twenty-five years a Captain of artillery in Europe in the service of the Dutch Republic. While he was content with his lot he regretted not having offered his services to the Persians, where he felt he would have risen further. As it was, he was still no more than a subaltern in a Merchant Company. "Conditions in Persia are becoming more and more turbulent," he said. "You are brave; I suggest you go there to seek your fortune." I replied that lacking any military experience I could not possibly hope to do as well as he. He offered to teach me sufficient about fortification and drill to seem to be a good officer to the Persians, who usually presided over an undisciplined rabble. I accepted his offer with alacrity and gave up the idea I was beginning to develop, of returning to the Cape. I told the Commandant of my genealogy, since in Persia it should make me more than a mere foreign adventurer. He had little faith in the tale, but to me it was evidence that I was as noble as the most ancient family in the Empire. "Far from his home country," he opined, "a man's worth depends on what he can do. You have some money, offer your services to the Shah of Persia under what title you please; he will judge you for what you are at the time. In the first place you will have to go to Persia as a merchant in order to get an introduction."

From that time on, I stopped thinking of myself as a country peasant. I took on the dignity of our ancestors, as revealed in the genealogy, and resolved to match them in status and fortune or perish in the attempt. Kind M. d'Imberbault, the Commandant, spent whole days together teaching me, and I learnt with a capacity which astonished him, although in fact he did not have very great technical knowledge. People exaggerate the difficulty of the science of fortification, he said, but to be a competent engineer it is really only necessary to have good sense, based on some sound principles. When it started, fortification was largely a work of instinct, and Vauban and Cahorn merely built on established foundations. Common sense suggests the superiority of acute angles over right angles, and curved walls over straight ones, when fortifying redoubts and encampments. The obvious uses of ditches, breast work and banks gave rise to the trenches, fascines, gabions and mantelets of the military engineer. Irregular terrain dictates the disposition of fortifications. The difficulty of approach during a siege led to the development of mines, which again evolved to suit the nature of the ground. Room for manoeuvre during active service has dictated that armies are split into brigades, battalions, columns and platoons. It is only necessary to have a good eye and a good voice and to understand those whom you command, to become a great leader if you have the necessary spirit and audacity.

Though I did not believe everything M. d'Imberbault told me, he instilled a spirit of self-confidence, even cockiness, which stood me in good stead on many occasions. Everything he said was useful. But nothing helped more, in the new world in which I was to find myself, than the drilling and management of battalions of four hundred and eighty men in all conditions, from six to thirty on all sides, or in groups of sixteen and twenty-four depending on the terrain or whether the action is offensive or defensive. These are the little secrets of the infantry which I was to use with advantage in the service of Nadir Shah and Mohammed Shah. It was due to him that I also developed other manoeuvres, in Persia and India, which made me a not inconsiderable exponent of military tactics in the east. The old Commandant took his teaching so much to heart that he made a table pierced with enough holes to hold a battalion of peg soldiers, and iron rods to move them, so that we could pass whole days developing our tactical skills.

    Two Company vessels were preparing to buy Persian silks at Gombroon or Bandar Abbas, and due to set sail on 18 October 1729. One of them put in to Malacca and had orders to take me on board. M. Master had been allowed to write one letter to me, which I received just before leaving. This kindly old man thanked me for my generosity towards his relatives (in stating publicly that I had left Batavia of my own volition), and together with his good wishes for my future success he sent a magnificent present of provisions for the journey and a pair of the most beautiful pistols I have ever seen. He concluded his letter by telling me that the resemblance of his legal heirs to me was their best recommendation. I parted from M. d'Imberbault with tears in my eyes. He gave me a gun which I still have, and a fine Swedish sword, which I gave to M. Durant of Marseilles when he promised to seek news of my dear brother. Whilst I was at her house, I had bought from Mme. Kalb a negro slave, who developed an attachment to me. As I left to make my fortune, he secreted himself with my goods on the boat, where he was later discovered.

    For a long time the weather was calm and we travelled only ten leagues in twenty four hours. Near the Maldives, however, the wind got up, and we made way with as much cheerfulness as speed, coming in sight of Bandar Abbas on the 23rd December. At the sound of our cannon Company officials put out in a dinghy and came aboard to tell us that there would be no silk that year because the Afghans, forced from Isfahan by

Shah Thamasp, son of Hussain, had withdrawn to Shiraz, where, knowing they could not hold it, they were pillaging the city and killing the inhabitants. The Afghan leader Ashraf, who had reigned since 1725 had come from Shiraz after suffering a setback in two great battles, from which he was not likely to recover. Despite their attempts to dissuade me I determined to land in Persia, and the Captain, who had orders to let me disembark where I would, did no more to influence me. We rowed to shore at the break of day. Arriving there I knelt and kissed the ground, crying: "In this country I will make my fortune, or die in the attempt."

Bandar Abbas was deserted when we landed, the warehouses of the Factory were empty and only the Director's house was furnished. From what M. d'Imberbault had told me, and the Agent confirmed, about the energy and resourcefulness of the Afghans, I believed they could hold their own in the war. It seemed to me that the best thing to do would be to offer to fight with them. M. Vanderhine, the Director, suggested that I should take my baggage to the Afghan officer in command at the Fort and ask him to escort me as far as Shiraz, where I should present myself to Ashraf. The officer demanded two tomans, which amounts to about sixty Dutch florins, for providing me with ten men. I prepared to leave from the Company premises on the 26th December 1730, thinking we could set out immediately, but the leader of the ten Afghans asked me for the two tomans owing. It turned out that the commander had kept for himself the money I gave him, so I produced two more and we got under way. The appearance of these men did not inspire confidence, since they looked more like robbers than soldiers. I was therefore careful to be agreeable and to flatter them. M. Vanderhine had sold me quite a nice horse that I intended to ride. I suggested to the leader of the party that he might like to use the horse instead, and offered to carry the haversacks of the others on my two camels. Politeness pays, and these uncouth men responded by saying they would only set off if I rode on the horse. I mounted forthwith, and we marched in good order. At the first halt I felt I should offer to share my provisions, but this time it turned out to be a mistake. At the sight of the bottles of fine Shiraz wine that the Factory agents had given me, my companions became strict Muslims and started to cast threatening glances at me and murmur amongst themselves. I was extremely afraid that they intended to set upon me as an infidel, and appeased them by a piece of diplomacy. When the bottles came to light I had them taken away by my black slave and pretended to be angry with him and scold him, to the point of making as if to strike him. What I had foreseen occurred. The ruffians were satisfied with my sacrifice, and while I had to be content with the food I had before me, they stole off one by one to sample the abandoned wine store.

The nearer we got to Shiraz the more horrific sights we saw. The countryside was burnt and strewn with rotting corpses. In the distance were ruins of villages, many of them still smoking. We were met by several platoons of Afghans, and I had to make presents to the leaders. I suspected some of these might be marauders from the Bandar Abbas garrison. I kept an eye on my escort, and noticed that someone had detached himself from one of the platoons and turned up amongst my ten. What could I do but keep quiet and be patient? That evening a man on horseback joined me, whom I recognised as the principle servant of the Factory at Gombroon. My escort was going to arrest him, but he struck one of them with his riding boot, another with his horse, all the time making friendly remarks, and passing between them, arrived at my side. "These rogues are up to no good", he shouted, "You have been diverted from the Shiraz road." When he had dismounted he told me his story. "I know how things work here and I shall be a useful companion if you let me join you. Your decision to try your fortune in Persia has inspired me to do the same. I have been with the Company at Gombroon for fifteen years and my career is not getting anywhere. I am the only clerk with a good knowledge of Persian and Banian. The directors make use of this but don't promote me. I am owed two years wages, so I took this horse and equipment instead - they can't complain. I will do all I can to protect you from the danger, and if you make your fortune I hope you will reward me."

I embraced my new comrade. His company was a great blessing to me. He was thirty years old and had been brought to Gombroon by one of the Directors from the boat on which he had been a cabin boy. The idea was that he should serve as an apprentice and learn Persian. He had surpassed the expectations of his master; Persian and Banian (an Indian dialect which merchants from India and Turkey use as a lingua franca) were now as familiar to him as his mother tongue. He was, moreover, very strong, forceful and enthusiastic. "If you ask me", said he, "you should get your negro to ride one of the camels and we will spur on our animals and take our leave of the escort, who look like a bunch of cut-throats. I know a route to Isfahan which I have been on many times, and I fear your companions more than any we may meet on the way. Why have they left the main road? Why did a similar troupe fire at me an hour ago? Allow me to get rid of the rascals."

To my shame, I was at first suspicious of these attempts by

Frederic to separate me from my escort. I imagined that he had resolved to rob me and proposed to do so in the absence of witnesses. With this thought in mind I said the following morning would be time enough to do as he suggested, when we would have the whole day in front of us. "So be it", he said, "if that is what you want. You do not know these people as I do, but at least follow my next advice. Stay awake during the night and keep your negro to one side with the camels. As for me, if I sleep it will be with my eyes open, my pistol and my gun at the ready and my arm through my horse's reins."

"Let us do better than that", I replied, "If these people have evil intent they will act when they think they can take us unawares. We can pretend to sleep, pretend to snore, and at the first movement from one of them we will get up and leave."

"I am afraid," retorted Frederic, "if they do move we will not be able to leave without a fight. However, yours is the best plan available now that we have no other choice."

Our people chose to camp under a palm tree. I said I was disturbed by the bad smell and the snoring of the camels, and put them a little way off with my slave, who had orders to keep a close watch on them, and Frederic gave an explanation of my actions to the Afghans. But when we said we wanted to remain with our horses they became sullen and stubborn. I began to believe we really were in danger. We leant against the palm and our ten Afghans settled in a circle around us. After about half an hour, we were snoring away, pretending to sleep heavily. That acted as a signal to the villains, who picked up their arms and got to their feet. I had no wish to find myself at their mercy, so shouting to Frederic to watch out, I leapt behind my horse, which shielded me from them and, firing one of my pistols, jumped into the saddle. Frederic was no less quick to mount, and we galloped towards our camels, which my slave had speedily prepared on hearing the disturbance. The Afghans were fearful and did not dare to follow us.

At the end of the following day we happened on a large troupe of Afghan cavalry marching straight to Shiraz, and a moment later a courier galloped past making for Bandar Abbas. Frederic opined that something special must have occurred to make a courier hurry like that, and he felt that we should march with the cavalry corps which we saw in the distance. I allowed him to have his way. After an hour we came to the cavalry camp. Frederic told me that we would soon be out of danger, the commander was undoubtedly a senior officer under whose protection we would soon be in Shiraz. No sooner had he said this than we heard the sound of hooves behind us. We turned and beheld four horsemen with drawn scimitars, which they flourished over their heads. Frederic recognised them as Persians and cried that they intended to encircle us and cut us down. When they had done so they would excuse themselves, saying they believed us to be spies. "Dismount", he said, "and if they continue to come on, shoot without asking questions. It is well for us that they are Persians." He leaped to the ground as he said this, and I followed suit. Our two shots killed one of them and wounded another. The two who remained turned and fled, while we redoubled our pace towards the camp. We got to the advanced guard without further ado and Frederic asked to be taken to their commander. While the officer was drawing up a detachment to take us, someone took the loads from our camels and piled them on the ground. This looked dangerous, and Frederic shouted at the men while one of them made to pull me from my horse. An officer restored order, however, striking the man who accosted me with the flat of his sword. We were forthwith taken to Zeberdest Khan. He was the General in command. Since the death of Nasrulla, to whom Mahmud owed his victories, he was the only officer the Afghan cavalry was prepared to serve.

Neahmed Zeberdest was Persian in origin. When very young he had been travelling with his father in a caravan, and fallen into the hands of Afghan bandits. One of them had adopted him, given him an education and trained him in the arts of war. He soon excelled at this occupation. For a while he was in the service of the Moghul Emperor, and obtained some knowledge of European military practice, especially of artillery, as a result of meeting Portuguese gunners. He was a fine man and, for Asia at least, a very good officer.

The previous year he had defended Kazvin against Thamasp and his general Kouli Khan, and he left Takht, to which he had withdrawn, to take command in Shiraz, which Thamasp and Kouli Khan were preparing to attack. Zeberdest liked Europeans and spoke well of the Portuguese. He was learning French, a little a day, from an iron-founder from Noményin Lorraine, in whose company he spent most of his free time. They were together when we asked for our audience and he sent his friend to enquire what our business was. The Frenchman was overjoyed at my reply. After having welcomed us he left but returned shortly to present us to the General, who, at our approach deigned to raise himself from the cushions upon which he was sitting cross-legged. Mindful of the advice of M. d'Imberbault I introduced myself as a French gentleman who had come to Persia out of curiosity and a love of adventure. I said I had experience with infantry and artillery, and despite my youth I was believed by Neahmed, who replied very obligingly in halting French. Frederic had already struck up a friendship with the master founder.

Having passed on our complaints about the loss of the baggage from our camels, Neahmed at once called the officer who had brought us to his presence and threatened him with the bastinado unless he retrieved all that had been taken. While waiting for supper, to which he invited us, he said that the fortunes of the Afghans depended on the outcome of the siege of Shiraz. I surmised, from the fact that he suggested I might join him is seeking service with the Indian Moghul if the City had to resist a siege, that he did not have much confidence in its defences. But I had notions of honour, and rejected the prospect of simply moving to the strongest side. Seeing that our host was relaxed after supper, which had consisted of some dried fruit and a large crock of Shiraz wine, I asked him if he would be so good as to provide us with a better account of the Afghan conquests than we were able to glean in Europe. The way I put this request made him smile. "We do not know each other well enough for such a conversation", he said, "I speak poor French and I must rest so as to be ready at day break." At the same time he asked M. Chomel, the iron founder, to put us up in his tent for the night. Having again expressed our hopes for the restitution of our baggage, we followed him and retired. "Ye Gods!" said M. Chomel, when we were in his tent, "You are fine one. Only two hours after you first meet the most exalted Afghan Lord in the land, respected and feared by everyone more than Shah Ashraf himself, you are already treating him like an old friend. You are a true Frenchman! But don't think your familiar attitude has offended him, he would be the first to tell you if it had. Meanwhile, since you want to know more about the Afghans I will provide some details. Few people in Persia know more about the subject than me. The prince of Georgia introduced me to it in Isfahan thirteen years ago. I had already passed seven years in the Palace workshops. I had seen Shah Hussain, been on friendly terms with one of the principle white eunuchs of the Harem and with a Georgian officer who had been in the wars against the Afghans and at one time their prisoner. I was at the centre of this nation for five years, though I am still treated merely as an artisan. I shall save you putting any more questions to Neahmed. As I am not otherwise occupied we can miss one night's sleep."

Before starting on his account, Chomel proposed that we have some wine, and we soon forgot that we had promised not to sleep. It seemed that no sooner did we become drowsy than a dozen soldiers disturbed us by bursting into the tent. They put down the remains of our baggage and assured us that no more was to be found. Although only a third had been recovered, Chomel urged us to appear satisfied, and Frederic said as much to the officer. Day having broken sooner than we intended, we made to go, putting off the account of the Afghans until we should enter Shiraz. There, Neahmed introduced me to Ashraf, who honoured me by presenting me with a calaate. This is a brocaded coat of a kind which Persian kings give as presents or witnesses to their esteem, to those accorded an audience. Having been declared Governor of Shiraz, Zeberdest made me Commander of the rampart artillery with Frederic as my Adjutant. I was more surprised than dismayed to find myself in such an important post with so little experience; it is not difficult to appear knowledgeable before people who know less. What was more worrying was my lack of language. The Afghans spoke a mixture of Turkish and

Persian and I did not care to learn that, seeing that, to all appearances I might not be long with them. When I heard that Persian was the Court language at Agra, as it was at Isfahan, I decided that was preferable, and with the help of Frederic and Chomel I soon learned enough to have no more need of an interpreter.

I am aware, my dear brother, that I have been speaking of the Afghans for some time, and that they are undoubtedly an unknown people so far as you are concerned. For the purposes of my story it is only necessary to refer to the events in which I took part. Some general information will, however, put them in perspective, so I am now going to provide a brief account of the incredible history of these people, who for so long lived in profound obscurity. I can tell you what I have learned of them from people here; their collapse and ruin have taken place, as I write, before my very eyes.

The Afghans originally lived in the Caucasus, from where they were removed to Persia by Tamerlane. Their nation was split into several branches between which religious differences fomented great animosity, kept under control when they were ruled by the Persians. The Afghan Abdalis were transposed to Khorasan, the Rasis or Shias to Hazerai, and the Sunni Afghans to Kandahar. I only have experience of the Rasis and Sunnis, who played the main part in the Persian conquest.

Sobriety, simplicity, acceptance of suffering, contempt for the easy life, even for life itself, characterized these two groups before their expansion. They enjoyed warfare, and not having chiefs of sufficient calibre to lead them under their own flags or those of the Persians or Mongols, they contented themselves with brigandage and pillaging caravans. Their arms were the lance, sabre, shield and dagger. They carried firearms for a short time after their conquests, but had no wish to employ them. When they fought they either won or perished in the effort. Their troops were divided into two corps, apart from the cavalry, called the Nazachksis and the Pekelhuvans, meaning, more or less, the Butchers and the Athletes. The Butchers were the elite of the nation. They formed the first ranks of the army and engaged the enemy first, creating a veritable turmoil. Undeterred by the size of their losses because they could not make them out, they were unstoppable and opened a way for the Athletes who followed them. When they had achieved their aim they wheeled to the sides and filtered back to form a rear guard (it is necessary here to point out that in the East soldiers usually fight in a single line). There they prevented anyone from fleeing and forced them to return to the battle or killed them if they resisted. A wound to the arm was not sufficient cause to leave the battle, the wounded person simply changed his sword to the other hand and continued to fight until victory was won or he reached the end of his strength. After the battle the wounded were tended with care, so long as they appeared to bear honourable wounds; if it looked as though they were received during flight from the field the unhappy victim was dispatched.

This firm resolution to win or to die in the attempt does not result in ferocity. The way they behave in victory would do credit to the best regulated society. Their prisoners are not enslaved. I have known many Georgian and Persian officers who have fallen into their hands and have been treated humanely. One, amongst others, was badly wounded and obliged to surrender to an Afghan, who at once asked if he could be exchanged for an Afghan prisoner. When the Georgian replied that he could not, the Afghan replied, "Well, stay with me for a year, do what you can for me and when that time is up I will send you home." The victor died during the year, and the Georgian thought he had lost all hope of being set free. He was wrong. The children of the dead man, having seen him weeping at the bier, took him to the judges before whom he explained who he was, and how long he had been in their father's house. He responded to everything, and told them of the promise the dead man had made to him. The children confirmed his story; after that the eldest son said "By the honour of our father, since he was an honest man and you grew to love him, we hereby set you free. Here is some money for support; return to your home."

A short section is left out here, which does not add materially to the narrative. Barely two weeks have elapsed since Daniel landed in Persia. With a rapidity to which he must by now have become accustomed, he is in Shiraz, a friend of the Afghan Prince Neahmed Zeberdest, and commander of the rampart guns. The Afghan Mahmud has usurped the throne of Persia. On his death it has passed to his cousin Ashraf, and Thamasp Kouli Khan is about the attack Shiraz in his campaign to wrest it back for Thamasp and ultimately for himself.

Kouli Khan left Isfahan on 17th January 1730 and took the road to Shiraz with an army of forty thousand men, while Thamasp took a larger force and marched towards Azerbaijan where the Turks were in control. On the news of these movements, Ashraf left Shiraz with ten thousand men to join a general called Seydal, who had brought from Kirman the survivors of the battle of Marschahkor, where he had been one of the commanders. With what he could get together of the scattered Afghan troops in the eastern provinces, Seydal could muster twelve or fifteen thousand men, and when the two forces came together the decision was taken to fall on Kouli Khan as he marched. Ashraf stationed himself in the mountains behind Zarghan, six days east of Shiraz.

Zeberdest Khan was now absolute master of Shiraz, and at once set about raising the defences. He had with him only six thousand Afghans - Abdalis, Rasis and Sunnis. But the inhabitants of Shiraz had been promised by Ashraf that he would make their city his capital. More than twenty thousand had been armed, and had agreed to cooperate in the defence. The ramparts were furnished with eighty cannons and full supplies of powder and shot. Zeberdest and Ashraf together had strengthened the fortifications of the city. A new wall was built thirty feet thick. It was an Asiatic mode of fortification formed from a palisade of trunks of whole plane trees set into the ground, the spaces between filled with compacted sand and rubble. Within it there was an inner wall that had been built up from ancient ruins and the stones from abandoned houses. At its foot was a fosse and strong palisade where crossbowmen and elite musketeers were to be placed. To make access more difficult the causeway over the river had been dug up, so that it would be flooded. This precaution proved useless, however, because at that time the river was low.

Kouli Khan arrived before the city on the 26th January 1731, about midday. Before nightfall his army had made camp. Seeing these preparations made so soon, Zeberdest regretted that the enemy had not been harassed on their march, and directed his principal lieutenant Udal to attack them with two thousand men at the bridge which the Persian commander was constructing over the river. I was ordered to accompany Udal with eight hundred townsmen, and after destroying the bridge, to retire to a dervish convent which formed a salient in the debris wall. Udal was more successful than we dared hope. The Persians who were at the bridge were displaced, and he then pursued them as far as their camp, which he set on fire. He retired with time enough to cause further damage to the bridge as his force recrossed it. I had taken charge of six small cannons which were at the salient. It occurred to me to set them up as a battery and train them on the bridge, which we could rake with fire at daybreak. As the convent connected to the defensive wall, we could easily bring up supplies and reinforcements, and this action could establish my reputation if I made a successful showing. I supplied my men with powder and ball, drew up four thousand townsmen armed with halberds, and having discharged a volley from my cannons I waited quietly for the arrival of the troops which I could see approaching the bridge. These were the second wave of Kouli Khan's forces.

 The Persians brought up eight cannons to threaten the convent. They fired, though with little effect because they were situated below us, and their infantry resolutely surged forward to the attack, scimitars in hand. We had the good fortune to repulse them twice. More reinforcements were brought up, however, who undertook a flanking movement, scaled the wall where it was poorly defended, and formed up to attack us from behind. My men concentrated at the convent were dismayed to find themselves cut off. They abandoned their posts and retired in disorder. I rallied them quickly so as to bring them back onto the rampart, and this time forced the Persians into the convent, which they prepared to defend. This action took about half an hour. I asked permission to attack them and force them out of my redoubt, and my manner was so pressing that despite the preference of some of his officers to wait until nightfall, Udal gave me authority to carry on as I wished. A battalion of Afghans was sent to join my troops. I took the lead, and making a turn to the right as if going back to the city, I traversed the convent wall to the north side which I felt was the weakest point. It was the hottest part of the day. Kouli Khan had retired to his camp, leaving only a detachment of five or six hundred men to guard the bridges. My party was in the convent before the Persians inside could re-form to defend it. All were put to the sword or fled in disorder, with the loss of no more than twenty men on our part. At the end of this engagement, however, a Persian officer whom I proposed to take prisoner, turned on me as I made to seize him and slashed at me with his scimitar. He caused a long cut to my belly, so that I had to hold in the vital organs with my hands. I was taken to the city, where for a month I had no other care than to recover from my wound.

In fact, this wound brought me much friendly attention from Zeberdest and his principal officers, who made frequent visits to me. Udal developed a tender affection, the first witness of which was a gift to me of the costly arms and armour of a chief whom the War Council had condemned to death for cowardice. I was starting on my recovery when it was announced that the Persian General had left his lines in the hands of Tafile Khan and taken his elite troops to find Ashraf, who threatened to force him to lift the siege. The commanders did me the honour of admitting me to their councils. The rubble wall had been completely broached by the enemy and the town was protected by nothing but its ancient rampart. The Zoroastrians, to whom Zeberdest had entrusted his mining enterprises, reported that Kouli Khan had begun tunnelling work there. They proposed we abandon the rampart in case we failed to neutralize the enemy mines, and build a new defence by the moat, which was now filled with water from former ditches. I was given the task of organizing this work. Zeberdest proposed the new plan less as a defensive measure for the city than to retain a strong position from which we could negotiate if we had to capitulate. He wished to be able to keep out Ashraf and Seydal if the battle of the plain went against them. Udal, who had the ear of the Governor, told me this. Having no mortars and lacking large cannons, which Ashraf had spiked before leaving Isfahan, the Persians would not be able to take the city by artillery assault, and their army was not strong enough to essay a frontal attack. I constructed a keep, putting into practice as much as I could of the lessons learned from M. d'Imberbault. The wall was formed of a multitude of angles, sometimes with re-entrants, sometimes salients, with horseshoe embrasures here and there, surmounted along the full length by double battlements. When a sortie to disperse the enemy failed, Zeberdest contented himself with mining the old rampart and withdrawing with his artillery to my new one. The water was drained from one moat to the next and we knew we could flood the last one when we needed to.

    The ninth day after Kouli Khan had departed we were visited by fugitives from Ashraf's army, who told us of the annihilation of his forces and the immanent return of the victor. The battle took place on the plain near Zarghan. The Persian general had detached a squadron of cavalry to pursue the vanquished Afghans, while he returned rapidly to Shiraz to attempt the complete destruction of the Afghan party. Zeberdest put to death the bringers of this vexatious news. Already he had conceived a plan which would efface the disgrace brought about by Ashraf, or would destroy him in the process. As ambitious as he was courageous, he proposed nothing less than to displace Ashraf, if fortune smiled on him. At nightfall on the 13th March he quitted the city with about four thousand Afghans and eight thousand loyal townsmen, who were told that the plan was to take Kouli Khan from behind while Ashraf attacked him in front. He left the command of Shiraz in the hands of Udal, urging him to keep up artillery fire and send out detachments from time to time to discomfort the enemy. "I shall find them on the march and unready for me" he told us, "and I have no doubt I shall prevail. That is the only way we can save ourselves."

That very night Tafile Khan attacked us in the city, with the loss of two sorties. The following day, having tunnelled into the ramparts he blew them up with frightening force, shattering the great plane trees that had been used to make them. But owing to the lack of skill of the miners, most of the rubble fell on his side and he gained little from the action. Some of the trees were blown as far as his camp, and the blast killed over a thousand of his troops who were poised ready to pass through the breach when it was opened. We added our fire to wreak further havoc, and realizing that he had nothing to gain from the engagement he retired to await the return of Kouli Khan. At midday on the 19th a field to the east of the ramparts filled with cavalry riding with all speed towards the city. These were some of Zeberdest's spahis. At first, Udal refused them an entry, but when they announced the defeat of Seydal and the approach of a victorious Kouli Khan, he let them in.

Tafile Khan must undoubtedly have received this news as well. No sooner had the horsemen entered than we noticed in his lines all the preparations for a major assault, and to our great consternation, we saw that as a result of the blast the water had drained from our moat into a subsidiary channel, so that it provided no protection. A multitude of Persian soldiers surged towards our defences carrying protective shields, and we felt our last hour had come. Udal gave the order to man the ramparts. I sprang to direct the artillery in this extremity. With one voice the officers exhorted the defenders to a last effort, so that we would be in a position to treat on fair terms if need be. Before nightfall the moat was dry and the Persians made preparations to scale the wall. We harried them with rounds of shot, but they kept up the work admirably under this fire, arranging ladders at the foot of the wall. With bravery bordering on madness, many of them climbed on each other's shoulders in order to try to gain an entry. The courage of the besieged was as great as that of the besiegers. We fought hand to hand, body to body, on the narrow top of the rampart. Some closed ranks so as not to cede ground, others determined to extend the ground they had won; it was a scene of frightful carnage for more than half an hour. At last, harried by fire from the turrets, which had assailed them throughout the attack, Tafile Khan's Persians withdrew, and we let them do so without daring to follow.

    Kouli Khan never forgave Tafile for this assault, which he had only undertaken so as to have the sole honour of entering the city. The general was no sooner in camp than he sent word that the inhabitants of Shiraz could hope for no quarter if they continued to bear arms against the Persians. The Persian officer who bore this message was taken to Udal's quarters, blindfolded and without being permitted to speak on the way. A council was assembled, and came up with these terms; that the city would be given up with its arms, munitions and shops, together with the womenfolk and treasure of Ashraf and Zeberdest, on two conditions. The first was a general pardon for the inhabitants of Shiraz and for those of the garrison who wished to remain in Persia. The second was for the freedom of all Afghans and their supporters then in Shiraz to withdraw to Kandahar with their arms and baggage. An hour later we received a reply. Kouli Khan refused the first condition absolutely but, faithful to a treaty of Mir Abi, he accepted the second, except as concerned the parts of the royal treasure of Isfahan which the Afghans had in their possession. The terms were agreed as soon as Kouli Khan gave his word to Udal that the punishment of the inhabitants would be limited to a ransom. We then had until the following day to make our arrangements to leave.

Several Persian officers entered the city to recruit to the service of the Shah any of our officers who wished to volunteer. I had intimated to the Persian who brought us the surrender terms that I could be a useful recruit, seeing the respect we had for the General. Udal, to whom I had confided my desire to stay in Persia, supported me. I asked, too, to bring what remained of the Zoroastrian force with me, together with a few of the braver townsmen who feared retribution by the victors. Accordingly, at the head of two hundred men I craved an audience with Kouli Khan to offer him our services. His pride as a conqueror led him to refuse this request, but he did assign me some quarters for the night, and I retired apprehensive of what the morning might bring. In the event, three days passed before he replied.

The only thing that gave me hope was that no-one had touched my possessions or harassed my men, who were still permitted to pass freely through the Persian camp. On the 24th the ransom which the city had raised to protect itself from pillage was to be distributed to the army. After receiving the order to attend I was very uncertain how I should conduct myself at this assembly. I consulted a Min Bashi or Colonel, with whom I had developed a friendship, as to what I should do. "The Khan wishes you to prove yourself." he said, "Be bold and put yourself in the line near me. When the distribution party reaches you say that you hope you have merited their attention."

Resolving to take his advice, I mustered my troop from their tents and dressed them under arms beside those of the Colonel, who had under his command a thousand soldiers. The disparity between our two corps was great. His looked like irregulars, while you could take the least of mine for an officer. Most were armed with good muskets, and those who had only halberd and sabre I arranged so cunningly that one could say that they were purposely armed in a different way. Kouli Khan rode along our ranks on horseback, and made gracious comments to each troop. He did not appear to distinguish mine from the others until each man had received the fifty abassis which were his due. But when he heard how I praised my men to the distributors he spoke, exhorting my men to live up to the reputation I had given them. He received my salute with a smile, and ordered me to his quarters after the review. That was a good sign, as he had given the same order to the other colonels.

When he was out of sight I mounted my horse. My new friend Muchid Bashi introduced me to his fellow colonels, and we assembled in a group in front of the Khan's tent. The Min Bashis arranged themselves in a row in order of seniority as he prepared to review them. When called by name, they said that they hoped to take arms against a more noble enemy than the miserable Afghans of whom they had now rid themselves. When he came to me he stopped a moment to look me over. I think I blushed and it seemed that my bearing made him feel that his inspection had made an impression. "Ah!" he said, "so you have come to join us." "My Lord", I replied in a firm but respectful manner, "I left Europe to seek honour in the service of the Shah, as a soldier under his orders. I landed at Bandar Abbas four months ago when the Afghans were masters of this land, and I preferred to fight with them to being their slave. Having got into Shiraz with Zeberdest, who allowed me to command his artillery, I had to fight valiantly during the siege, because you would not have wanted me as a coward and deserter. But as soon as you had shown by the terms you arranged with Udal that you respected those involved in the defence, I chose to forego his invitation to join him in seeking service with the Moghul of India. If you will accept me into your army I shall be your servant from that moment on, and shall live or die on your orders."

"Follow me", he retorted, "and I will tell you what I shall do." After giving each colonel a gold piece he urged his horse towards the city, accompanied by an old Persian noble, and he signed to me to follow him. "Was it you", he asked, when we reached the moat, "who constructed this new rampart?" When I replied in the affirmative, he asked me whether we would have resisted an attack there if he had refused our terms. "Yes, my Lord." I replied stoutly, "and we would have repulsed a second attack as we did the first."

"Was it not you", he continued, "who commanded the artillery?" Without giving me time to reply, he asked if Persian was spoken in my country. "If so", he added, smiling, "they speak it very badly. But why did you come to Persia?" When I naively replied that I had come to seek my fortune, he asked me why I hoped to do better here than in Europe. I replied that Europe was at peace at the moment, and that when it was at war there were many who could do as well as I. "You expected to find us ignorant?" "My Lord", I replied in Persian, "in a place where clothes and customs are quite different from those of Europe I expected to find people ignorant of things I knew but knowledgeable about things of which I knew nothing. What I know, if it is new, they can find useful. That is true above all of military matters."

The old nobleman asked me to repeat what I had said in Dutch, and he translated it for the Khan in his own exquisite Persian, so that he appeared satisfied. "Is that how you build fortifications in Europe?" he asked. "That is what could be done in six days. All Shiraz laboured on it - men, women and children. Such a work cannot have the style or solidity of a regular fortification. With more time and better materials I could produce a magnificent structure, with bastion, tenaille, caponier, ravelin, a covered way..." I came out with all the terms M. d'Imberbault had taught me, and I used them confidently, as if I had been a Vauban or Cahorn.

"You know how to construct", he said, "and you know how to defend, too, if it was you who regained the Dervish house after you were dislodged from it. What is your religion?" "That is unfortunate", he said on hearing that I was a Christian, "Muslims will not readily obey an infidel. Why don't you become a Muslim, or at least pretend to do so?"

"My Lord", I replied, "I could not live with my conscience if I were unfaithful to my religion. I pray you, be like the

Afghans. They gave me loyal service and did not question what I was." "I would like you to go to Kandahar", he told me, "and give me an accurate report on the state of their citadel. It should not be difficult for you to gain an entry, because you have no need to tell them that you have changed sides. I have already had the soldiers you brought with you dispersed among our Persians. Pretend you decided to leave. Go to Hamed Khan, who will give you further instructions. Serve the Shah well, and I will find you the fortune you seek."

On returning to my quarters I found no-one there. Even Frederic was gone. I made a great commotion and had my friend Muchid Bashi believe that the Khan had dismissed me. After spending an hour complaining about the injustice of this treatment, I took my leave, saying that I was going to demand my due from Hamed Khan, who appeared to have the ear of the General. In fact, when I had an audience with him he told me that the war against the Ottomans prevented Kandahar from being reduced at this time. The General hoped to be informed not only of its present state but also of the forces at the disposition of the Afghans, of the negotiations of Mir Abi with the Turks and the Moghul, of what the Afghans thought of him, and above all, whether there had been any reconciliation between the Afghans of Kandahar and their ancient enemies the Hazerai Afghans. "That is the task you are charged with", Hamed told me, "Kouli Khan has had his eye on you ever since Shiraz was ceded. Seeing the alacrity with which you put on a show of contempt, he judged you to be very capable for the task. Do not regret losing your troop of men. The rank of Min Bashi awaits you on your return, with an effective command in the artillery. I have instructions to provide you with twenty gold pieces for your journey, and a personal slave.

You shall have them now."

I took the twenty gold pieces, but I refused the slave and asked the old Khan to help me find Frederic. I also asked him to permit me to leave with Muchid everything I had brought from Shiraz, which constituted my worldly goods. "I shall do the first as confidentially as I can." he said to me, "As for your second request, that must be done for all to see. I am to hold, on behalf of the general, all your baggage and goods with the exception of your negro. Your slaves and horses are to be sold publicly. I will make good their value when you return. This is necessary if you are to be believed when you say you are dissatisfied with us."

Everything turned out as Hamed Khan had said. Frederic joined me before nightfall, and on the order of the General I found myself so divested of my possessions that we had to pass the night in the city. By taking these actions, Muchid caused me to loose all status. When I wished to say goodbye he turned me away, treating me as if he believed my disgrace would taint him. I appreciated his friendship for its true worth. Discretion had been the first lesson I learned from my experience of the Court. Despite his many proofs of friendship and support I was also sparing in what I told Frederic. I kept my true mission secret because the risks entailed were so great.

PART II

On Kouli Khan's behalf Daniel goes to Kandahar to gain information on Afghan plans. He returns to Isfahan, fights the Turks in Iraq, marries and becomes rich.

When the unfortunate Ashraf had presented me with the calaate I was advised by Chomel to be careful what I did with the white turban which was part of it. If I had imprudently worn it, my life would have been altered, as I would have had to undergo the operation which is the mark of the Mohammedan. I wore instead a military cap. To be suitably clad for my journey to Kandahar I accompanied this with Armenian clothes. I bought two camels, one for my luggage and the other for some cheap merchandise. Thus equipped I made my way cheerfully towards Rabal Emir, in Sablustan, on the frontier of Kandahar. But no sooner had we set foot in this little kingdom than we were set upon by a troop of Afghans against whom resistance would have been futile. Our lives would have been lost if I had not presented myself to be an envoy from Udal to Mir Abi. Frederic supported me by telling them of the damage they would do to their brethren recently escaped from Shiraz, in whose interests we were making our journey, if they did us any harm. These pleas worked, and they contented themselves with plundering the baggage on our camels. Frederic actually did think I was on my way to Kandahar to await Udal and continue with him to India. He was therefore able to speak with conviction, whereas he might have felt compromised if I had told him the truth. After the effectiveness of our first lie he dealt happily with other bands of lawless Afghans whom we met. We got to Kandahar with both our money and our mounts. There was general alarm in that city, where Mir Abi no longer had faith in his treaty with the Shah. Now that Ashraf was dead, killed in the mountains of Kasas with those who accompanied him on his flight, he assumed that Kouli Khan would soon arrive to take the Afghan stronghold.

As the Afghans from Shiraz had marched as an army, they had not yet arrived at Kandahar. When Mir Abi found I had taken part in the siege of Shiraz, he instructed me to lodge in the citadel, which he had made his palace. The usual constraints a stranger would experience in such a fortress were not applied to me. I was granted an audience the following morning, and passed the evening pacing the citadel walls, so that I could draw an exact plan of it when I had the materials to do so. The garrison was composed of five or six hundred members of the Prince's personal guard. About thirty cannon without carriages were disposed along the curtain wall, and about as many along the outer works. These last were professionally built, by a Portuguese engineer when the fortress was held by the Moghul. Since then, they had been extremely neglected, so that the place would not have withstood an attack by a professional army. Returning to the barracks where I had lodging, I wrote a description of the fort, after tracing with my pen as best I could the outlines of each of the fortifications. I resolved to get these sketches worked up by a draughtsman in Isfahan if I did not gain the necessary skills myself. My success so far had come from learning things like that.

After the third prayer on the following day Mir Abi summoned me. I found him sitting on a pile of goat skin cushions which gave little indication of his wealth. His clothes looked ragged. His turban was dirty, with a tuft of tattered herons feathers attached to it by a diamond pin. His kaftan was a dusty pink and he wore a brocaded shirt. Instead of slippers he had on a pair of Tartar boots. He was tall and well built, with a brown face, prominent eyes and an agreeable expression. Around him were four men dressed as janissaries with tight-fitting Tartar jackets and drawn sabres. Frederic was with me, and we were dressed in rich Armenian clothes as was appropriate for a meeting of such importance. The Prince rose from his cushions, approached us and presented his hand, then took us to an inner room where the floor tiles were covered in a magnificent Persian carpet worn into holes by the dust. He made the guards wait outside and placed us beside him on a sofa.

He commenced by telling us of his regret at the death of Zeberdest, whom he had loved tenderly, then went on to the message he hoped to convey, in his present difficult position. After that he began to speak with a passion which did not seem diplomatic of the difficulties caused by the death of Ashraf and the collapse of his forces. All the time he addressed himself to Frederic; because of my youth he could not believe that Frederic had been my second-in-command at the siege of Shiraz. To him, we both appeared to be fine men, and I accepted his mistake, until Frederic had the good grace to explain the position. When we had given a brief account of the siege he asked us what we thought were the present intentions of Kouli Khan and his master Shah Thamasp.

At this point I felt an inexpressible emotion at being accepted by this straightforward man while working for his enemies. It would have been no worse to deceive the Persians than to deceive him, and I believe I would have chosen to remain with him if I had felt he could prevail in the contest which was bound to come. I relied on Frederic to give his opinion while I composed myself. Upon reflection, my actions did not seem so culpable. Feeling more at ease I took up the story myself when Frederic had finished.

I told him that the intention of the Shah and the advice of his council must be to reduce Kandahar at least to the status it had under earlier reigns. The revolution had shown what the Afghans could do under an ambitious leader and he could not permit such a prince to control the city without risking a new uprising when the Afghans had recovered from their present setback. Mir Abi interrupted to say that as long as he lived the Afghans would not be subjects of the Persians, but that he would give the Shah such assurances as he needed that he would remain a friendly but independent state.

Having called for narghiles and coffee the Prince, in his turn, told us of the theft of a letter from the Moghul to the Shah by a band of Afghans who had attacked and massacred the envoys of the Moghul at the frontier of Kiablistan. The discovery of this document made him think of preparing one of his own to the Shah. I expressed interest in seeing this important document, which I conjectured would bring me credit with Kouli Khan, but he would not take the hint. After we had been three hours with him he dismissed us, and arranged that we should meet again the following day at the same time.

When we presented ourselves, as ordered, to the guards at the door, they demanded presents for the Prince. Last time, we had forgotten the etiquette, and were passed straight through because we had been summonsed. This time it was necessary to pay; Frederic handed over his silver watch. One of them took it to the Prince, who professed himself well satisfied and greeted us as before. He had the coffee and narghiles brought in and then fired questions at us about the Shah and his General. The conversation got round imperceptibly to the letter. "If this letter is no use to you, my Lord", I asked, "why not gain merit with the Shah by passing it on to him? It would be a mark of your affection, which he would like. On the other hand, if you can gain an advantage for yourself and your nation, and give yourself a strong ally, you might instead negotiate with Delhi along the lines of your agreement with Ashraf."

My remarks had the effect I hoped for. Mir Abi ordered a clerk to bring the letter and invited us to examine it with him. Here is the translation I made of the original.

> *In the name of Allah the eternal and all-powerful*
>
> *The most noble and invincible Muhammad, son of Alam Bahadur, of Aurangzeb, of Shah Jahan, of Jahangir, of Akhbar, of Humayun, of Babur the Sword Carrier of the Prophet, of Sheik Omar, of Abu Said, of Tamerlane, most favoured of the All-High, sovereign of the great Kingdoms of the earth, Master of Delhi, of Lahore, of Kandahar, cities innumerable, King of Kandahar and of an infinitude of other kingdoms wherein are cities, fortresses and castles with men, arms and treasure that the Great Envoy of God alone can count.*
>
> *To the most glorious and powerful Shah Ashraf, exalted as the moon in the night sky, greatest among equals, lover of goodness, profound in wisdom and celebrated for his valour,*

salutations from our Imperial city of Lahore, the 12th in the month of Regiab, in the year 1142 from the Hegira (December 1729 of the Christian era).

Having learned from messengers to our Imperial abode that the Kizilbashis, whom you have made your subjects by force of arms, have revolted against you, we offer you with our cordial and fraternal affection, aid from our invincible army to reduce them to the obedience, which they owe to you, as to their King, since you now stand in that relation to them. Following the precept of the Prophet, who exhorted us to help the afflicted, we will send to your aid the elite of our valiant soldiers under the command of the most able and courageous Omrah Mameluk, whose sword cuts like fire, without asking anything of you except that as simple justice requires, you give back the City and Kingdom of Kandahar, which the Kings of Persia, your predecessors, unjustly and fraudulently took from us. Our faithful subject the Omrah Mameluk will be at your orders on the frontier of Kandahar, at the head of one hundred thousand Children of the Prophet before the month of Safer next. We wish you boundless prosperity.

After the recital of the letter I suggested to Mir Abi that he should intimate to the Shah that he would never enter into an agreement with the Moghul, since that Prince only wished to recover Kandahar. When he said that before doing so he wanted to consult Udal and the other officers who had escaped from Shiraz, I suggested that he could expect their fidelity. After all, they were not Banians, whose business required that they travel from India to Persia on business, who would resent being kept in ignorance of something which so signally affected them and would inform the Shah in order to gain their favour. I went so far as to offer to take his commission to Isfahan myself. "Perhaps", I added, "this service will put me in favour with the Shah, and if he should settle me in Persia, you would have in me a faithful and discrete servant to promote your cause."

This last part of my discourse clinched the matter. Seeing that he was persuaded, I decided to recapitulate the perils to which I would be exposed on behalf of the Afghans, for no other reason than my affection for his people. I made him understand that if I was capable of infidelity, it would not prejudice his cause; passing on the details of the letter would help my standing in Persia, and he should not ask anything but that I communicate it. In the end, I persuaded him. He said I should be his secret agent in Isfahan, and gave me four days grace to be on my way. I asked for eight, which I said were necessary to avoid any suspicion that I had an agreement with him, to which the Chiefs in Kandahar might take exception; but really I only wished to have time to see the city and make an assessment of its strength and morale. During the four days on which he insisted, I learned enough of Kandahar to provide Kouli Khan with a report which he found satisfactory. I left with all I could have wished for. Frederic, astonished at seeing me prepare to return to Persia, rightly suspected that I was not letting him into my confidence, and was annoyed about it. But he was mollified when I told him that it was of the greatest importance to me that I put off sharing my secrets until we got to Isfahan, and I emphasised that when we arrived there I would tell him everything.

When we got to Seistan we learned that Kouli Khan was with his army in Khorasan, where he was waging war without quarter against the Abdali Afghans, whom he was preparing to besiege in Herat. I got close to him by crossing the regions of Gor and Gasna, and arrived shortly after Herat fell and all those who were Afghan had been put to the sword. I made my report, which earned me much praise. But at the sight of the letter, a copy of which I furnished him with, the Khan went into transports of delight. "You have made me a signal service," said he, "that will not be forgotten; I shall reward you beyond your expectations. You must leave today for Isfahan and report to Hamed as soon as you arrive. When you have done that, return and tell me what he says."

Without knowing it I was to be the bearer of tidings of a new revolution. During the short time I was in the camp, I was able to guess that he plotted something to the disadvantage of Shah Thamasp, by the disrespectful manner in which the officers spoke of him, and particularly because of the whispers going about, concerning a young Khan, said to be the second son of Shah Soleiman, who had disappeared from the Harem. Obliged to leave before these rumours became public, I went with a confused picture from which I could make nothing except that the ambitious Kouli Khan was trying to raise himself higher than he already was, although, next to the Shah, he was now the highest in the land.

I arrived in Isfahan on 26th July 1732 and went straight to

Hamed Khan, who was acting Chief Justice. The perusal of my dispatches interested him greatly. "You have been a long time", he said to me, "getting from Herat to Isfahan. The Shah will be here in a few days with a strong force. I will do everything to help him, but if we are not careful our actions will lose us all our friends."

My eyes opened wide at this announcement. I did not know how to respond because I was not privy to the secret, as he believed me to be. Realizing his mistake he quickly changed the subject. Instead, he pretended we were talking about the obstacle the General wished to put in the way of the peace with the Ottomans. "The Shah", he continued, "had already signed the treaty when the letter from the Khan arrived with his objections. Can you imagine that after such a great victory, which opened the way to our conquering the Turks, the Shah would think that we could buy peace by ceding several fine Persian provinces? It is a dreadful mistake which we cannot correct. I am now going to write a reply to the Khan."

I was not taken in by the old minister. But seeing that he could well resent it if I appeared to have guessed something he had no wish to tell me, I retired without letting him know I understood. The Shah was then at Farabad, a fortress about two leagues from Isfahan, where he had installed a few eunuchs and women, well removed from any thought of the peril which threatened him. He sent orders for his army to the Khan, and had no doubts about their being obeyed. The dispatches, of which I had been the carrier, asked Hamed Khan to assure himself of the support of the people of Isfahan, and prepare them to receive the General, who planned to dethrone the son of Hussain and put himself in his place. Stories of his pretended descent from ancient Sophis had been put about by messengers to find out whether they would be believed and to measure how much and where he would have support from the army. Nobody took the fable seriously, and he abandoned it without giving up his plan.

Since Hamed made me wait two days to take his reply, I was able to observe his conduct. At different times and under different pretexts he assembled in his palace all the Persian officers in the city who had been dismissed by the Shah after the peace treaty was concluded. Most owed their advancement to the General, who had promoted them and bestowed on them titles formerly reserved exclusively for noble families. In the absence of these families, whom the Afghans had destroyed, titles were awarded on merit, and men of humble station had become rich and powerful as a result. Having lost their military positions they were poor again. Hamed Khan soon found them willing to support Kouli Khan, whom they respected as a commander. The conspiracy grew in the capital, as it did in the General's camp. I carried the news to the audacious Kouli Khan, ten days march from Isfahan at the head of forty thousand men. I was received with every expression of eagerness. Having read the dispatches he came out of his tent, took me by the hand and asked if I had noticed anything odd in the capital.

"My Lord", I replied, "I had no wish to pry into a secret to which you had not made me privy. But if it is your wish to assume the crown, and poise your sword over the head of the son of Hussain, you have but to say the word. There are over a thousand officers and ten times as many dissatisfied soldiers, who would acclaim you with delight."

He regarded me fixedly in silence, then letting go of my hand he ordered me to mount a horse and follow him. "I remember", he said, "that I promised you employment, and that Hamed gave you hope of the rank of Min Bashi. I am now going to promote you in front of the army. You will enter Isfahan with Aradik Khan and Muchid, and summon the officers and men of whom you spoke. Form from them, in any way you choose, a troop of a thousand men. When I arrive I will see to the rest. While there, stay with Hamed Khan, whom I love as a son. Be secret and diligent, and nothing will stop us."

The army of Kouli Khan was put under arms. The Khan addressed them saying that the Shah had ordered that they be disbanded. The officers had prepared their soldiers for this development. There was a unanimous acclamation of the General and imprecations were hurled at the name of the son of Hussain. The General surveyed the ranks and called to them, asking if they would follow him to defeat the Ottomans, of whom he spoke with contempt. On their cry of assent, he said they must have another Shah, and that Thamasp had a son. When the General proclaimed him Shah Abbas, his name rose from the ranks in a great cry. The tumult was quelled by a distribution of money, and the army was ordered to draw up in battle order to march on the capital.

It was after that I was created Min Bashi. The Khan allotted me one of his tents, where I could receive my new companions. We passed the night together, drinking and smoking. At daybreak I went to the tent of Aradik Khan, where I found Muchid. An hour later we had assembled a squadron, and with them we set out at the head of a cavalry corps of three thousand men. We were in sight of Isfahan by the 6th September. Aradik Khan picketed his troops in front of Farabad, where the Shah was still installed. Muchid, three other Min Bashis and I entered the capital. There I went to find Hamed to give him a letter from the General.

   The Chief Justice introduced me to a group of revolutionary officers and until the 15th I was employed discussing matters with them and forming my own troop. Hamed gave me thirty gold pieces for their arms and subsistence. On the 21st, Kouli Khan made camp half a day's march from Farabad. He told the Shah of his arrival, and said to him that his brave men who had served the Shah so well required payment before being discharged; he had brought them here, telling them of the Shah's generosity, and expressed a desire that the Shah should review them, in the company of his paymasters. The Shah seemed to be roused from his drowsiness by this, and to realize the intentions of his general. Himself master of dissimulation, he invited the Khan to come to Isfahan for discussion of the most suitable amount of money to distribute. While this message was being sent, he left Farabad and returned to the capital. But there everything conspired towards his downfall. Muchid and his companions had formed their companies, as I had mine. Two other revolutionary Min Bashis assembled with theirs. Numerous high officers who commanded well-armed battalions had their troops disposed according to a plan conceived by Hamed, so that in less than half an hour they held all the principle points of the city.

   On the morning of the 23rd I received orders from Hamed to post myself on the avenues of the Maidan, near the mosque of Mehedi, to train my twenty cannons on the palace gates, and to advance at midday as soon as a detachment of cavalry entered. I carried out these instructions to the letter. Aradik Khan, who commanded the cavalry detachment, about three hundred men, entered the Harem without being disturbed. He spoke to the Shah, saying that the army wished for his presence. This unfortunate prince had done nothing for himself since parting from the Khan. In response, he now left the capital followed by his treasurers with many camels loaded with gold and other valuables, perhaps hoping that these goods would satisfy the army. Having departed, he was never to return. The ambitious Kouli Khan used the occasion to give a feast for his supporters, and the following day brought Thamasp's son from his Harem on a litter and had him proclaimed Shah in front of the army. He then took the young monarch to his palace. The title of Ichmedaulat, or chief minister, which Thamasp had conferred on him did not seem to him to confer sufficient authority, and he announced himself Guardian of the young Shah in front of all the principal officers of the Court and of the army assembled in the Maidan, and assumed the reins of government under the title of Kausoli Khan, Prince Liberator. By popular acclaim he had been named Feli Nimed, Benefactor of the People, but he preferred the former title.

The first acts of the Liberator concerned internal affairs. Shah Thamasp had revoked an order, established by Ashraf, which had submitted the Persians themselves to the will of citizens of other nations. This change had potential repercussions, however. The Persians were a minority, and putting them in command tended to unite the rest against them. It was important that these new masters did not impose too heavy a burden upon the others. TheKausoli's edict stated that all who contributed to the welfare and glory of the state would be equally dear to the sovereign, regardless of their racial origins. He wished to consolidate the country so that all the forces of the state could be brought to bear on his great project, the war against the Ottomans. His policy, contrary to that of

Abbas the Great, was that there should be no divisions between peoples in cities or villages. Whilst there was a strong ruler no harm had been done by sectarian differences, but under Soleiman and Hussain half the population was pitted against the other. The disputes were nourished by the proclamations of the Imams and Mullahs, whose strongest allegiances were to one or other saint or martyr. The Kausoli ordered the clergy to prepare a calendar of saints, whose cult he would approve, and to concentrate their minds, he closed the palace of the Grand Cadi for a fortnight, so that they were without women or servants until they had prepared their scheme. The Council presented their calendar with despatch. It was published throughout the land, and it was forbidden, under pain of disembowelment, to worship at the shrine of any saint who had been proscribed or to interfere with anyone worshipping at one which was listed.

However, since the intention of Kausoli was only to get rid of the factions and not to interfere with questions of conscience, he permitted any form of worship within doors. So far as Europeans were concerned, he confirmed the concessions to the Catholics and allowed those of other sects to build churches as they wished. This tolerance was inspired by a Flemish renegade, who had left the Ottoman camp the previous year to join him at Tabriz. His true name was Vandren, but in Asia he had taken the name of Soleiman. He was a good engineer, and because the Kausoli knew that his knowledge was much greater than mine, I came to be removed from the artillery service which he had originally proposed for me.

This Vandren had brought to Persia the entire artillery company which had been at Kausoli's disposal since 1733, sufficient to mount one hundred cannon. They had been used in the two last campaigns against the Ottomans and in the wars with the Afghans and the Moghul. Among others, they had with them a German from Hamburg called Roth, an excellent bombardier and a particular friend of mine, and a Frenchman, Bonal, who acted as engineer to the gunners. He arrived at the camp in Tiflis in 1735. It was he who constructed the bridges over the Indus in the campaigns against the Moghul. Both were extremely rich, having found favour with Kausoli before my flight from Persia. I met Vandren again in Delhi. He was dressed as a Persian Grand Master of Artillery, and much feared and respected by the army, although reviled by the courtiers whom he subjected to military discipline like junior officers. The Kausoli used the opportunity provided by the dethroning of Thamasp to dispose also of the remaining Persian nobles. Some he had murdered, others were banished, he put out the eyes of several, and rewarded his friends with their confiscated property and goods. Tafile Khan, whom he had never forgiven for the attack on Shiraz, was one of these, and I received most of his wealth.

 I remained in the house of Hamed Khan because he had plans for me to marry Fatme, one of his daughters. Although to this date I had paid no attention to them, the ladies of this land are the most beautiful in all Asia. Concerned only with making my fortune and obeying the precepts of my religion, I had not taken advantage of the privileges of the victor. Nor had I considered contracting a marriage to someone of modest means, a marriage which in the custom of Persia would last only so long as my wife appealed to me and which would then be broken off simply by return of the dowry. Before marrying me to his daughter, Hamed wished to know whether my single state was due to coldness or timidity, so without my knowing it, he arranged one of those marriages of which I have just spoken - to a charming young Georgian girl of whom he had heard me speaking admiringly. I was completely astonished one day to find her in one of my rooms, accompanied by a black eunuch. This monster prostrated himself on my arrival and congratulated me on the happiness I had in store. Curiosity made me enter the room, without thought of the consequences. I saw the delightful Janna, dressed in a caftan, or robe of filmy muslin, that permitted me to see the lightness and beauty of her body, made by nature as if for pleasure. She had cast herself negligently on a sofa, her head resting on one hand in the attitude of a person in a deep sleep. I approached this pretty scene. Georgian education does not instil European decorum. Janna had been brought up a Georgian and she felt more strongly that she was a girl than that she was a Christian. We did not speak much of this last quality, but were immediately overcome by a feeling that we were made for each other. I was weak and believed myself in heaven, soon forgetting that to make a good marriage one should first find a clergyman. My old patron was very pleased when he learned of my response, and started to make preparations for the alliance with which he proposed to honour me.

I soon opened my eyes to the predicament I was in. After having fallen so far for Persian customs it would only take another moment of weakness for me to become a Muslim. The idea filled me with horror, and I replied to my patron in the terms of a man who, regretting that he has fallen, is determined to mend his ways. I could only see two choices, to abandon Janna and wed Fatme, according to the ways of my religion, or to legitimise my relations with Janna. The interests of my career indicated that I should take the first course, but I had fallen in love with the Georgian and could not bear the prospect of a separation which would be desolating to us both. The old Khan could only laugh at my distress, and gave me a month to make up my mind. If I was content with the pleasure of being with Janna, he added, I was welcome to seek my fortune where I could find it. "But take my advice. She is not bound to you, any more than you are to her. Your house could become a place of torment, if she chooses. Consider that while making up your mind."

The old Khan had a son about eighteen years old. He was a pleasant young man, newly parted from the company of the eunuchs who were his tutors, and I was pleased to continue his education by teaching him the little I had learned. In a way unknown in the East I introduced him to Janna as a third in our private apartments, as I would in Europe a relation or a friend of my wife. We ate together, and we passed the evenings playing games, chatting and smoking. Young Mehedi was more often in my rooms than with his father. Janna treated him with no more than politeness, while her loving attentions to me increased from day to day. I was so satisfied with this arrangement that its ending was all the more unexpected. On the first day that I was parted from my tender Georgian I attended a dinner given by some Dutchmen from the Company Factory in Isfahan for the new Director from Gombroon. Feeling somewhat unwell, I left the table and made my way back to my house long before the evening's entertainment was due to end. Entering through a little garden, which Hamed had subdivided from his for my convenience, I noticed that the window of my dear Janna's room was open. The demon of jealousy assailed me, causing me to lurk against the wall in order to see whether it was simply to obtain fresh air that my innocent risked catching cold. In spite of my repeated desire to go and see what was inside I was patient enough to wait two hours like that. Eventually the sound of the sentry roused me and caused me to look more intently at the window. Janna herself was framed in it, attaching a rope ladder to the casement, and a moment later I saw with my own eyes something I could not otherwise have believed. Young Mehedi appeared and after receiving an affectionate kiss from Janna descended the ladder and disappeared with all speed through the gate to his father's garden, which he appeared a little surprised to find closed. According to the precept of the Persian poet, who recommended sleep before vengeance, I went to bed without visiting my love. When she appeared inquiring after my health, I told her I was a little out of sorts.

That experience made me think. From the resolution that I should confront the pair with their infidelity, and crush them with my outrage, I passed to a feeling of contempt, of amusement, even, at the effrontery of it, and finally of embarrassment at the thought of the old Khan reminding me of what he had said. After this lesson, I was impatient for the visit I must make to him. I went to my patron with a genial expression, affecting to be free and relaxed.

"Janna has accepted her dowry, My Lord", I said to him, "after I presented it to her with many expressions of indulgence. I am free and will accept, when it pleases you, the honour of alliance with you, and give you my word that I will marry my wife without any conditions."

From the way he replied I had a feeling he knew what had been going on. But I had no wish to enquire further into something I found mortifying. This event changed my prospects, and I was now impatient to become his son-in-law so long as the Persian ladies were made in a different mould from the Georgians. The old Khan made sufficient comment on my experience.

"You will often be deceived", he told me, "if you conduct yourself with women in Asia as you would in Europe. Europeans have a variety of interests but Persian women, perpetually restricted, have no other activity but love, and they are violent. Imagine what passion is generated in the Harem, coupled with hatred and contempt for the monsters who are in charge. I have seen them descend to the most loathsome flattery of the black eunuchs, hideous creatures that they are, in order to further their secret amours."

On thinking about the remarks of the old Khan I formed a plan of marriage which I believed would not run counter to my religion but at the same time would save me from the opprobrium and rage inevitable in a union in which there was no trust. In a country where I had no minister to consult I felt I must be my own judge and council. I promised myself that I would be faithful to the wife I married, never taking companions or rivals, but that I would only consider myself married so long as she took the same course and remained faithful to me. Seeing that education and temperament worked against this, as the old Khan said, I resolved to consider divorce well and truly merited by any infringement of the strict rules of the Harem. My insistence on this arose from the same source as the violence of the desires of eastern women. My religion taught me to bestow my affection jealously upon one object of love. Be that as it may, I married the young Fatme, and despite these thoughts so little compatible with affection and love, I was happy in my marriage with her. Whether through wisdom or understanding, through skill or the limited opportunity for unfaithfulness, the question of divorce never arose. It only remained to have a son for my household to be perfectly happy and content. The doctors in India opined that the reason we had no issue lay with me. Certainly it seems to be true that the climate, and the temperament of the women of Asia, make polygamy necessary to be sure of heirs.

   The Kausoli left to join the army on the 6th March 1733. Already the commerce and wealth of Persia was improving, as a result of the wise rulings which had been made since the deposing of Thamasp. Following the advice of Vandren, an Inspector General and a Provost General for the whole of the kingdom had been appointed. The first was charged with overseeing and repairing the roads and caravanserais, while the second ensured their security by rigorously enforcing the laws against theft promulgated by Shah Abbas the Great. The former Persian nobility, destroyed by Mahmud, Ashraf and the Kausoli himself, was replaced by the creation of a new nobility, drawn largely from the army. The edict stated that in a land acquired and recovered by force of arms it was necessary to have a military nobility. They were appointed, according to the Kausoli, not for long service but strictly on grounds of ability. Those who only owed their rank to the deaths of their comrades and their good character had no right to a position, which must be reward for blood shed and perils sustained in the service of the state.

   Mahmud, Sultan of Turkey since 1730, sent an emissary to Isfahan who threatened Ottoman vengeance on all who helped to depose the son of Hussain. The Porte did not believe that the Kausoli could wage a foreign war, given the state of the country. The Regent did not disabuse it of this error. Having incarcerated the Ottoman courier in the castle of Zaroutaki, he wrote to the Divan in Constantinople unexpectedly proposing negotiation. It was only on the day of his departure to the army that he raised his mask and, releasing the emissary, sent him on his way with a letter containing a declaration of war. We expected the Turks to be on the defensive. Their forces were commanded by the old general Topal Osman, renowned for his ability and tireless energy. Although he was a cripple, as his name indicates, he was a fearless commander in battle, being carried on a litter into the midst of the fighting.

The Kausoli could count on one hundred and twenty thousand men, drawn from the conquering armies, and in eight days he had them prepared. The plan of campaign was to establish the forces on the Tigris so that Baghdad could be attacked after the Persian territories in Kurdistan had been recaptured. Informed of our departure from Tabriz, Topal Osman sent an order to the Pasha of Baghdad, to draw up all his forces before us, burning and ravaging ground which we abandoned. This would have caused us great distress, because it would be difficult to provision ourselves. The Kausoli resolved to prevent it by marching straight on the Pasha with the elite of his cavalry, a corps of sixteen thousand fanatics, whose baggage was loaded on camels. The march took seven days. The Pasha was unable, or did not wish to avoid the resulting battle, which he lost completely. The Kausoli pursued him towards Baghdad, where all the army had arrived by 27th April. A siege was undertaken and pushed with much energy so as to take the city before Topal Osman arrived, as there was no hope of successfully defending ourselves against him. But the Pasha, who had a large force with him, conducted his defence so well that after three weeks we were scarcely better off than we had been at the start.

Topal Osman was two days march from our camp on the 16th May. The Kausoli raised the siege the following day, and pretending to advance towards Topal Osman to fight him, he avoided contact by means of a forced march which took us to Kurdistan. He directed the rearguard action himself, and was defeated on the 23rd May. The withdrawal of the rest of the army was more like a rout. All would have been lost if Topal Osman had found in his janissaries the ardour of our spahis, but his infantry refused to follow, and without it he did not dare to engage in full-scale battle. On the 8th June we camped at Alback in Turkestan, to the east of Bitlis. The Kausoli tried to instill the old confidence in his army. He reviewed the troops, consisting of forty five thousand infantrymen and twenty two thousand cavalry. He gave presents to the officers and distributed pay to the men. Their spirit rapidly revived. Topal Osman, having reinforced his army with all he could gather from garrisons and from the country, was at the head of eighty thousand men. In addition, he had the support of the Tartars, commanded by the Beylerbeg of Asia. He made his camp six leagues from us at the foot of Kusbeg Daghi on the 24th. The Kausoli determined on a battle, but Topal Osman, who counted on our forces running, was not prepared to risk it. There was much skirmishing every day, in which he often had the advantage, until on the 3rd July he decided to engage in a general action. We found ourselves at a disadvantage, and unable to get the enemy commander where we wanted him. On the 4th July the Kausoli marched with all his cavalry with the intention of investing Kars. Arslan Khan, the son of an old comrade, commanded the infantry, and he was ordered to march on Bitlis. That was a dangerous move. The idea was to place such an attractive bait in the way of Topal Osman, that he could not resist attacking. When the Turkish general, who had good spies, realized that our infantry was marching between his lesser camp in the mountains and his grand army at Kusbeg, he believed he could subject it to fire from both flanks and was sure of its defeat.

Soon after the Kausoli set off, Arslan Khan approached a Kurdish prince who could muster four hundred men and resented the encroachment of the Turks on his land. The Kausoli was counting on his support and hearing that it was offered he ceased his forced march. He retraced his steps during the night, and on the following evening was at the back of Topal Osman, who was preparing to attack Arslan. By a movement to the left, he got to Kusbeg, where he saw his chance and fell on the enemy's advance guard, avenging his setback of the 23rd May. Topal Osman was hoping at least to defeat Arslan; instead he found he could neither advance nor retreat. Arslan dug in before the Turks, and to amuse himself, made an offer of surrender. Osman rejected all thought of negotiation, but with an excess of concern for his troops, contented himself with waiting instead of falling on us in the open country, persuaded no doubt that he would eventually prevail without combat. In the middle of the night of 9th July the Kausoli gave an agreed signal and Arslan brought his troops from their trenches so that they would be ready for battle at daybreak. After our cannons had fired into their ranks we fell on the Turkish infantry, who recoiled at our charge. Each Min Bashi was at the head of his men, whom he marshalled as he chose, and orders were given that we should force the day. My men were mustered in two battalions, each five hundred strong, twenty across by twenty five deep. Most were armed with the long Afghan half-pike. We fought the janissaries at the closest quarters imaginable. Their musket balls killed many of us and after the first charge we might have been totally annihilated had it not been for a successful assault by Kausoli on the Beylerbeg of Asia, whose forces staggered under his attack. Koja Nasir Bashi Khan, seeing us exposed to mortal danger again while our General reformed his troops, did not wait for orders but moved in to our left. He was on foot, sabre in hand marching fearlessly at the head of his men, and I joined him with mine. At the same time the Beylerbeg of Asia fell back in disorder towards Topal Osman. We realized from the ragged knots of janissaries whom we encountered that the disorder was spreading, and a great cry of victory arose from our ranks. The ranks of the enemy opened, we subdued those in front of us and created a frightful carnage. Topal Osman disappeared, nobody came forward to replace him, terror swept his army, there was nothing but butchery until nightfall. All the Turkish artillery were destroyed, along with the baggage train, which was pillaged. The Kausoli set off in pursuit of those who fled the field and did not return until the 12th, followed by the prisoners he had taken.

The prisoners from this encounter were distributed as domestics among the Persian peasants of Mazenderan and Gilan, where there was a great scarcity of labourers in the fields. Their lot was softened by an edict which deprived their masters of the right of life or death over them, and restricted corporal punishment to twenty strokes with a cane. Judges were installed to oversee their actions and when necessary, to punish them; wounded veterans were given these posts. To forestall the abuses that these new slaves could perpetrate, the punishment of impalement was decreed for anyone who attempted to take the life of a Persian in order to facilitate an escape, and perpetual slavery for anyone who attempted to rob his master. The captive families were sent to Khorasan, where they were put in the households of those who had followed Mohammed Khan, and of some of the Abdali Afghans who were exterminated.

After this military action I passed the rest of the year in the capital, where my father-in-law arranged that my men should be stationed. I was completely happy in the bosom of his family which had adopted me unreservedly. Personal friend of a man who had the ear of the Kausoli, esteemed by the army where I was not without merit, hero to my troop, from whom the Kausoli had selected a number of officers for his Guard, and several newly created nobles, admitted by my father-in-law to confidential discussions on matters the Kausoli put to him for consideration, knowledgeable about the great affairs of that man and confident of the measures he took for their execution, I came by a considerable fortune with expectations of an infinitely greater one. But Providence dictated that I should hardly have time to enjoy my prosperity, before the seeds of my disgrace should begin to grow.

A Dutchman named Saran, dissatisfied with the Company in the service of which he had worked on the Malabar coast, decided to present himself to the Kausoli as a man capable of opening up a new commercial enterprise in Persia. He produced a highly chimerical plan which, in order to work, required a more powerful maritime presence than that of Holland in the Asian seas. He argued that the isle of Hormuz, Bandar Abbas, Muscat and Basra could become the commercial conduit between Europe and central Asia, that by means of canals cut beside the Tigris and Euphrates in the straits where the two rivers had defiles and cascades, merchandise could be carried as far as Aleppo and from there to the Mediterranean. On the other side one could use camels to transport goods across Persia, bringing them to the Caspian Sea, where they would have access to the vast territories of the Czar in central Asia. This madman said that by agreement or by force the proposed route could excite the interest of the European powers. Proximity, he said, would favour Persian vessels carrying goods to India, and the Moghul would be persuaded to grant to Persia an exclusive trading agreement. The outlay for the Persian traders would be minimal, profit from the Indian trade would be great. The English would be happy with the Mediterranean maritime trade when they saw that it would be best to leave the Asian seas to the Dutch, and the success of Persia in her war with Turkey would put her in a position to dictate what terms were required, - amongst others, that there should be a minimum number of Persians on board their vessels so as to develop them as a maritime force in two or three years.

This ridiculous project struck a chord with the Kausoli, who admired wild and reckless schemes in others. The fantasies of Saran fitted in with his own secret desire to wage war on the Moghul, and the recent campaign had given him such a great contempt for the Turks that he did not doubt he would prevail.

He asked Hamed Khan to advise him on Saran's proposals, as he did on all subjects. Vandren, a better courtier than me, pretended to approve of the project, although in fact he thought it absurd. He knew he depended on the Kausoli for his success, and he did not believe that he would suffer when the Kausoli realized the truth about the project, because it was no crime to be less clever than him. As for me, I was not able to betray the confidence of my benefactor by praising something I realized he would one day regret. The project was accepted despite my reservations. My misplaced candour made the Kausoli assume that if I did not approve of it I would be happy to see it fail.

Daniel continues to fight valiantly for his adopted leader, helping him to usurp the throne. After being acclaimed Shah, Nadir sends Daniel on a mission to Constantinople, but rivalries cause his fall from favour. He escapes to his former friends in Kandahar. There he defends the city against Nadir until another escape, this time to India.

The campaign of 1735 opened with the siege of Erivan, which the Kausoli undertook with an army of eighty thousand men, whilst Arslan Khan and Prince Nerov entered Georgia, where they blockaded Tiflis. Ibrahim Pasha held Erivan with nine thousand men, and Abdullah Koprulu, who had succeeded Topal Osman commanding the Turkish troops, moved to his aid with all the Ottoman forces. The Kausoli wished to take the city before he got there, since he was not prepared to dig in. He had some little pontoons built which could be thrown over a moat. As soon as the army had taken up positions they were put across the Kurs river, a stream which served as moat on the east side of the city walls, and leading the infantry himself, he broke through and dislodged the garrison, which retired to the Keep with hardly a fight.

Our cannon were disposed facing the rock on which the Keep was situated. For six days there was continual fire from the sixty great guns, which shook the foundations of the redoubt. Ibrahim rejected the ultimatum he received, and the Kausoli again commanded the assault, which was again successful. The Pasha was killed and the day was won after fierce sword combat. I was wounded twice by shot, but only lightly. After eight hours rest, the Kausoli decided to march to Erzurum. Hussain Pasha, who commanded there, also controlled the marauding bands in the mountains of Aran, through whose defiles we had to pass. The Bashi Khan, leading an advance party, was surprised and beaten back, and we entered the gorges before knowing of his defeat. The army then found itself in very great peril. Scarcely was our advance guard well into the valley than we were assailed from end to end over a distance of two leagues by a rain of stones and musket fire. We could easily see where they came from, but the distance of the enemy was so great and his position on rocky outcrops overlooking the valley so impregnable, that nobody dared to mount an attack. I was with Arslan Khan in the advance guard. I asked his permission to attempt to scale the heights to get behind our assailants, and this he agreed to. Not to be outdone, another Min Bashi got permission to join me. We scrambled with incredible difficulty up the rock in the face of a cascade of boulders thrown down from above. My companion was killed by one which caused him to fall the full length of the cliff. About a hundred men from our two troops were lost, but finally we were masters of the heights and displaced the irregulars by attacking them from behind. Others along the summits were seized with fear at our success and retired, so that the army managed to pass the night in the defile unmolested. I received an order from the Kausoli to come down from the mountains because he proposed to return to the plains. We reversed the column and marched towards Erivan to face the Turks there. I was welcomed by the Kausoli as one who had rendered him a signal service. Not content with giving me a gratuity of a thousand tomans, half of which was to be distributed to my troops, he promoted me to Bashi Khan before the army, and, presenting me with a beautiful and finely equipped horse, he invited me to assume the functions of my new dignity and lead the advance guard.

We received news from Constantinople that the Sultan, taken up with his war against Russia, had ordered Abdulla Koprulu Pasha to make peace with us. The Kausoli, always a fox rather than a lion, wanted to gain all the advantage he could. Having sounded out the Pasha, he proposed a meeting at the little town of Elmiazin on the far side of the Giakuni river. The Pasha sent Muluk Kasenadar, his army treasurer with the Pasha of Baghdad, while the Kausoli and I were accompanied by Abdul Bashi Khan. There were four points he wished to discuss, the first and the fourth to be secret. The first was an exhortation to Sultan Mahmud and his successors to annul the religious disputes fomented by clerics on both sides, which kept Turks and Persians at war, and to assist the Kausoli to foster commerce across the two Empires for their mutual benefit. The Sultan should receive three thousand Persians on his boats to train them as sailors, then return them within two years, or in case they died, replace them with European slaves. The second article referred to reestablishing the frontiers of the two Empires as they were in the reign of Shah Abbas the Great, with a renewal of the treaty made between him and Amurat IV.

It was stipulated in the third that Persians who were prisoners or slaves in the Ottoman territories were to be given up, and none would be taken again under any pretext, with the exception of girls for the seraglios of the Sultan and his grandees, while prisoners and slaves transported to Persia during the war would remain where they were. According to the last the Kausoli, under the name of Nadir Mirza, was to be recognised as the legitimate successor of the son of Tahmasp, and after him his sons, should the young Prince die. In return, the Kausoli would do all he could to assist the Sultan in his struggle with the Muscovites and provide twenty thousand horsemen for the wars against the Austrian Emperor, but above all, help him in reducing the Arabs, who had again revolted.

    The Kausoli received dispatches at his camp, which told him that Abdulla, feeling that we were disposed towards peace, wished to discuss the treaty with Shah Tahmasp at Tabriz. He became extremely angry at this news. "What?" he said, "We are masters of their land and they dare to ask that we give them ours!" He immediately gave orders for the discussions to be terminated. The Pasha of Aleppo, a violent and superstitious man, reproached us for not dealing with them in good faith and called down a thousand imprecations upon our army. We found their forces had crossed the river Kars a little above its confluence with the Aras. The country they occupied was between the two rivers, which were about eight leagues apart and enclosed a stretch of land sixteen or eighteen leagues long ending in the fortress of Kan, beneath which Abdulla Koprulu had made camp.

    Like Topal Osman, Abdulla knew how to delay. From his impregnable position, he insulted us in all sorts of ways while we could only respond with cannon shots. As we could not cut his supply lines it was necessary to revert to our first strategy and control the road to Erzurum. We got within sight of that city when we learned of the surrender of Tiflis and the decampment of Abdulla. Our army moved to the left, having the Euphrates on its right, and at the end of the fifth day's march we were attacked by Abdulla's Tartars. We made our camp at Kirkuk, three leagues above the Euphrates. The enemy established itself at Mirjas, with the river on its right. At dusk Hoja Nasir and I received an order to go round Erman Daghi so as to have our backs to the Armenian mountains and fall on the left flank of the enemy army in the morning. We carried out this order to the letter. In six hours we had moved six field guns and eight thousand men over five leagues along rough tracks. We settled in, after placing sentinels along the ridge dividing us from the enemy. Although we could not see whether the Kausoli had carried out his intention of attacking at sunrise, Hoja Nasir wished to indicate that we were in position behind Abdulla by firing our six cannons. I consented with misgivings; if we were too early we were in danger of being overcome by the whole of the left wing of the enemy. We were nevertheless in good spirits and, in the end, fought until four in the afternoon on a broad front with our troops and artillery.

After this first encounter Abdulla regrouped his forces. He judged the troops on his flank to be the best in our army, since they could engage him effectively after a punishing night march, and formed his men into a rectangle with the narrow side facing us. The infantry were in front and formed the centre of the body in a series of little battalions, with the cavalry forming two reserves on either side. This arrangement was entirely defensive, and it was employed with great effect to withstand our attacks, visiting frightful losses on us. He had eighty guns which kept up continuous fire and we were fighting until nightfall. In this action we lost three thousand of the eight thousand men we had at the start. For his part, the Kausoli lost proportionally more. We would have been even more afflicted if Abdulla, who had fewer casualties, had attacked us at daybreak, but either because his men refused or because he did not dare, he spent the night putting the Euphrates between himself and us. With incredible effort he constructed rafts, on which the cannons and their ammunition were taken across the river, while his Tartars and spahis swam the torrent and the janissaries and other infantry crossed as best they could behind the horses. By daybreak we saw that, without being able to do anything about it, more than twenty-five thousand men were waiting their turn to cross. A gunshot wound to the body and another in my arm prevented me from joining the pursuit, which took place over nine days during which there was a series of skirmishes which could almost be described as battles. Although the Kausoli had the advantage he did not stop Abdulla marching towards his former camp at Kars. Within sight of his goal we engaged him in a general battle, and the unfortunate commander, five Pashas and the elite of the janissaries perished on that field. Chargers from Diabekir and some ten thousand prisoners taken for Persia were not the least return from this victory. The season being too far advanced to attempt the siege of Kars, the army withdrew, some of it to Tabriz, others to Persia and others to Georgia by different routes, having recovered all the territory the Turks had taken from us.

  The poor state of my health prevented me from making any preparations for the next campaign. Instead I became acquainted with the secret measures by which the Kausoli was preparing to become Shah. The young prince appeared not to be long for this world. While waiting for him to die, the Kausoli wished to be sure that people did not think he was hastening his end. He relied on the goodwill of the army. A treaty was concluded on 27th February between the Turks and Abdul Bashi Khan on our side, so that in fact the army was not mobilized. Instead the Kausoli convoked an assembly at a little town called Shoul Mogan in the desert of Iraq, consisting of mullahs, deputies and representative of the muslim clergy, Armenian patriarchs, Georgians, governors of provinces and cities, tribal chiefs, justices and so on, drawn from the whole of Persia. It was a veritable convocation of the Establishment of Persia. Attendance was compulsory under pain of death.

On the 24th March the army was put under arms ready to be reviewed by the Kausoli. Two hundred thousand tomans was to be distributed, and support for the general was guaranteed by his generosity. There was a wild shout. "We need a Shah who can command in the field", they cried, "No-one can surpass Nadir. Allah and the Prophet preserve him."

The officers had engineered this expression in his favour, which was news to the others assembled. The Kausoli pretended to be embarrassed and upset at the tumult. He said in response that he was only prepared to reign if he received the assent of the convocation he had convened, and he asked the army to put the question of choice of Shah to the Establishment. They did so by threatening to kill anyone who disagreed with them, and soon found support was unanimous.

Immediately after this proclamation of the 29th March, the new Shah sent Abdul Bashi Khan to Constantinople as an ambassador to ratify the peace treaty, requiring him to wait at Erzurum until I had time to join him. My instructions were to work with him as his second in command, but to be alone responsible for the fourth article, which had been put to the conference at Malatia, namely the status of Nadir as Shah. However, the main object of my mission was to meet all the Europeans I could in Constantinople who could be of use with respect to Persian affairs, especially where these concerned the military.

For his part, the Shah wished to see how the ambassador from the Sultan would react when he was received in an audience chamber decked out with military rather than royal furnishings. Tambour, timbales and trumpets replaced the usual court symphony, and the place looked more like an arsenal than a court apartment when the ambassador was received. I learned from my father-in-law why he adopted this course. The Shah had grandiose plans, which required that the Turks faithfully observed the treaty, and he wished to test their patience, which he judged was necessary for peace, and to instil fear for a Prince who would seem completely committed to war. Although surprised at what he found, Ahmed Koprulu advanced with pride towards the throne, where according to Persian usage he should prostrate himself. When it was apparent that he was not going to do so, the chief Black Agha, who was master of ceremonies on these occasions, barred his way. He required him to make three obeisances, and arriving at the throne he knelt before handing to the Shah the letter from his master the Sultan. He then made a speech in which, as in the letter, all the details of the treaty were specified. After the audience, the Shah divested himself of his dignity, as it were, and talked familiarly with the ambassador while taking him towards the room where a celebratory banquet had been prepared. This took them to the other end of the Harem, so that the ambassador could see that the rest of the palace was no longer arranged as it had been under the previous Shahs. Instead of eunuchs, who would have been in attendance under the Sophis, there were four thousand of the finest Georgians and Persians perfectly armed in the European manner except for their uniforms. To the Shah's satisfaction the ambassador noted the difference.

As I had no special function in the ambassadorial party I was able to explore Constantinople when I arrived there, and get to know it in detail, which I thought would stand me in good stead with the Shah. Abdul was received with all possible ceremony. He made his salaams and immediately entered into the ratification of the treaty, despite my telling him that we had yet to discuss the fourth article. I recounted my objections to this course of action in a letter to my father-in-law, but my strong protector died before the ratification. Abdul, who with Vandren, objected to my reservations about the Saran project, prevented me learning the news on the pretext of sparing me sadness at a time when I needed all my wits about me. He received the order to return on 17th October, and had a final audience on the 22nd, resolving to depart immediately after. I offered to remain behind to continue discussing the fourth article with the Turkish diplomats, but was rejected. We disagreed completely over this, and each wrote to Isfahan about the matter. Abdul's letters were dispatched to the Shah, while mine were held back. On the 5th December I received a fulminating missive from the Shah, in which he reproached me for hindering Abdul in his negotiations by creating perpetual distractions. He ordered me to remain where I was to deal with this affair, with no other authority than Agent at the Porte, and said how angry he would be if matters were not settled within two months.

I was extremely agitated on hearing this. It was easy to see who would lose. Abdul could say what he liked to the Grand Vizier and the other ministers of the Sublime Porte, to whom I was unknown. In Constantinople, I would be compromised, and Abdul's access to the Shah would allow him to harm me in that quarter too. Inevitably I should have to carry the blame for his failings in the negotiations. Resigned in advance to my disgrace, I hastened to salve what I could of my fortune. My only real friends were my brother-in-law Mehedi, and Frederic. The first had been brought up to render blind obedience to the Shah, and the latter was advantageously fixed in Isfahan, where he now had a large family. I therefore had to accept that fear of disgrace might make them less than willing to help me in such dangerous circumstances. As much for them as for myself I resolved not to put their friendship to a test they might fail. It would then be doubly distressful if they abandoned me. Pretending to need money in Constantinople, I sent to the Director of the Dutch Factory in Isfahan for a draft for a thousand tomans, and wrote to my brother-in-law asking him to change what I had in the way of gold and silver plate into cash, asking him to pay it to the aforesaid Director against his draft, and to raise whatever else he could from my other assets, to be sent directly to me. "I can only influence the ministers at the Porte", I said, "by means of lavish presents, and I shall get my possessions back when I am successful here." At the same time I wrote to Frederic, asking him to raise from an Armenian merchant in Zulfa fifteen hundred tomans owing to me as my commission from the dispersion of slaves and transplanted families. After the setback my fortunes had just sustained, I planned to return to Europe with this money.

   Instead of doing what I asked, Frederic and Mehedi told me that the Shah wanted me in Isfahan to give my own explanation of events, and had issued an order to that effect following the disgrace of Abdul. Mehedi had paid a thousand tomans from his own pocket to M. Norpéen, the Factor, and Frederic sent on his own account one hundred sultanins. Both refused to realize my effects, for fear of being implicated with me in any future disgrace. Muchid Bashi Khan, with whom I had only been on formal terms since I had appeared to turn my back on Abdul, wrote to me by the same express to warn me that I would be undone if I returned. I also found in his letter a note from Roth, who told be that the rumour in Isfahan was that I had been corrupted, like Abdul, by bribes from the Grand Vizier. Having been ignominiously sent from the Shah's presence, Abdul used all his allies to work to my detriment. The new Shah had already shown signs of arbitrary despotism, so that Roth believed that I should certainly suffer if I returned.

Roth had nothing to gain from my flight, so I accepted his advice as from a friend and weighed up what I should do. I remembered the old punishments, the least of which was to have one's nose and ears pierced, one's eyes put out, or to be disembowelled. The very idea of courting such risks made me tremble. On the other hand, six years of wealth and status made me equally unwilling to live as a fugitive. I was assured of the thousand tomans from M. Norpéen, provided I could turn up to get them. If I then fled, however, people would suspect collusion between him and me; he would be compromised and after eight years of effort and peril I would end up as poor as I was born. I had with me five or six hundred tomans. That at least was something, but how to be certain there was not a Persian in Constantinople charged with detaining me if I were to sell up my goods? I was paying dear with these tribulations for my years of prosperity and pleasure!

Finally, I decided. Afflicted equally by the risk of torture and the fear of penury, I left Stamboul on 4th March 1737 for Persia, and took the usual commercial route to Erzurum, with twenty slaves and six Persians in my entourage. There I stopped, pretending to be ill. I payed off the Persians, who were eager to get back to Isfahan, and in their place I sent Abdala, the faithful negro whom I had bought from Mme. Kalb, with orders to find out what the news was in Tabriz and to join me at the Capuchin Convent there. I had hopes that the good fathers would recognise the friendship with which I had always treated their compatriots in Isfahan. The day after the Persians left I put by baggage and affairs in the hands of an Armenian who had been acting as steward, asking him to travel slowly on account of the two fine Turkish horses which had been presented to me in Constantinople. I then set out, dressed as an Armenian monk, mounted on a dromedary hired from a driver who accompanied me riding another. In this way I entered Tabriz without being interrogated by the Guard, and I went straight to the convent of the Capuchins. There I met Father Damaze, whom I had known well in Isfahan, which he had recently left. He was surprised and pleased to see me. His reception was so cordial that I did not hesitate to tell him of my scheme for disguise. He sympathised with my plight. Through the Governor of Tabriz he had learnt that the dissatisfaction of the Shah with Abdul was related to his political activities, since the Shah wished to know how weak the Turks were, and how likely they were to remain at peace. But I was not in a position to gain much from this knowledge. When Abdala arrived his account of his journey raised new fears. Apparently, the Governor had interrogated the six Persians about me, and when ordering them to continue to Isfahan he gave them a message for Aslan Khan which did not speak well of me.

I pressed Father Damaze to give me a monk's cassock so that I could go to Isfahan incognito, but the good man said that, although he would risk his life for me, he could not profane the cloth by putting it on the back of a Protestant. I found that well said, and felt my secret was in good hands. Abdala bought two camels from our camel driver, and I eventually left for Isfahan in my Armenian disguise. We saw the six Persians in front of us in the desert of Iraq, but managing to avoid them, we arrived in the capital without misadventure. I went to see M. Norpéen on the 9th May, talked to him and found that he viewed my situation more seriously than Fr. Damaze. Since there were no Dutch boats at Bandar Abbas on which I could leave, he advised me to choose some other means to get away while there was still time. "You could reach the Indian frontier dressed like that", he said. "Don't put it off. I can provide a letter of credit for your thousand tomans with an Indian merchant. You can collect in Lahore or Delhi, or Surat for that matter, as you wish. I suggest you don't show yourself to your brother-in-law or any of your other friends - you would put them in danger. The more people know you are here, the more likely you are to be discovered, and those known to have kept quiet about your whereabouts would be punished."

Although I saw his point, I felt that I must contact my brother-in-law, and also Frederic. I suppose this was more impulsiveness than confidence in my safety. It cost me a lot to give up my home, and sometimes I felt this fear was all a false alarm. I arranged through an intermediary to meet Frederic in his garden at Zulfa. He arrived late, and I only needed to feel his coldness to realize that it was a mistake to meet him. "You seem to want me to go down with you", said this man who had formerly worked so hard on my behalf. "Do you not know that there is a warrant out for your arrest? Why have you come here? I wrote to tell you to stay away. Your brother-in-law is now a Min Bashi and one of your enemies. His daughter is going to marry Aslan Khan, who has offered him the command of your troop. His sister is to be married to your mutual friend, Muchid Bashi Khan, who will ensure that all your goods are confiscated and get the credit you have with Yussuf the Armenian. If you stay in Isfahan you will be discovered, and I will be punished for not turning you in. Abdul has suffered, and says you alone are responsible."

"Enough!" I said to my craven and unfaithful friend. "I shall leave Isfahan this evening, and never come back. I plan to return to Constantinople. You have my authority to obtain fifteen hundred tomans from Yussuf. I owe you twenty which you sent me. I give you one hundred and eighty in recognition of the help you have provided. Let me pay the thirteen hundred remaining in jewels."

He raised his eyebrows at this. "If your brother-in-law asks me for the fifteen hundred which he knows Yussuf is holding", he said, "how am I to obtain it?" "I do not know." I replied, suppressing my anger and contempt. "Thanks to your generosity my only choice is to fly. Adieu, my dear Frederic, I wish you better luck than I have at the moment."

I went back to the house of M. Norpéen, taking diversions and doubling back on my route as I went is case Frederic should follow me. I was well enough aware that my former friends wished to be rid of me, as a result of jealousy or greed or both. More than once I resolved to go to the Shah to expose their designs. I would be justified, I said to myself, and my boldness in seeing him would convince the Prince. But when I considered the details I felt overwhelmed by the difficulties. How to ask for and obtain an audience, given that those who surrounded him knew he had ordered me to be detained? I would be arrested and those who wished me ill would have their way. Roth had been won over, Muchid and Mehedi had betrayed me, and Frederic would only hold back from handing me over to my ambitious brother-in-law because he coveted the fifteen hundred tomans.

My doubts even extended to the generous and obliging M. Norpéen. I started to feel that he would give me a false credit note for India, which would not be accepted there. When you are betrayed by your friends you begin to see traitors everywhere. M. Norpéen's kind attentions calmed me, however. I realized that he was an honest man, and hoped that with his help I would be able to find, in India, the fortune which chance had so malignly taken from me in Persia. To allay my doubts about the letter to the Banian in India, he offered to give me the equivalent sum in gold, and pretended not to have noticed my mistrust. He invited me to stay in a private apartment in his house until there was a caravan ready to leave. From there I could observe the effect of news of my disappearance and know whether Frederic was traitor enough to tell anyone where I was planning to go. In a few days I felt such a hatred for Persia I no longer regretted having to leave, and started to look forward to visiting the lands of the Moghul.

The war which had been declared against the Afghans of Kandahar meant that the usual route was closed, and merchants who wanted to go to India had to take an escort and travel through Herat and Samarcand. To spread the cost, they waited until a large party could be formed, and that delayed things until 13th July. I passed the time with M. Norpéen, who treated me as if my disgrace had not occurred. The Shah ratified the treaty with Turkey, Abdul returned to Isfahan, my wife was married to Muchid, Mehedi had command of my troop, and Frederic kept possession of my fifteen hundred tomans. When M. Norpéen spoke to them, these last three said that unfortunately I had been robbed and killed by bandits in Kurdistan on my way home.

I was more conscious of these losses than of the other aspects of my disgrace. But reflection consoled me and inspired in me a mad plan to end my enforced idleness. I decided to go to Kandahar.

Although I never thought to see him again, I had occasionally written to Mir Abi to tell him my news and send him little gifts. He had replied with expressions of friendship and offers of service with his forces. Nothing would be easier than to persuade him that I had always been a faithful friend. At least, I hoped that was the case. I joined a caravan in the outskirts of Isfahan, in European dress which made me unrecognisable even to M. Norpéen. As I had brought the most precious of my belongings with me from Erzurum, I loaded a camel without making any more purchases. I hid one thousand tomans in gold among them, and arranged for Abdala to ride this camel, while I put myself on another like a poor merchant.

When travelling with a caravan it is wise to put the things one values most with those which appear least important. Planning to get to Kandahar, we left the caravan when it entered the land of Gasna, and were in Afghan territory on 28th August. I left off my European dress for Persian attire, with a white turban so that I might pass for a Sunni muslim; this was to ensure my safety up to the gates of Kandahar. The sight of the sad fortifications which the Mir Abi had erected filled me with joy. The Shah would imagine a siege to be easy, and I flattered myself that I could be troublesome to him; this would avenge to some extent the difficulties he had caused me. When I was admitted to an audience with Mir Abi I found Udal, my old commander, with him, and his presence contributed to my warm reception. With great effrontery, I lied to the Prince, telling him that I had written twice about plans the Shah had to annihilate the Afghans, but that it appeared the carriers of my missives had been killed on the way by robbers. I told him of my zeal for his service. Udal also assured him that he had seen me risk my life for the Afghan cause, so that he offered me the position I had held under Zeberdest in Shiraz. I listened carefully to his instructions. Udal, knowing what I had done at Shiraz, showed me around the new fortifications and repairs to the citadel. I criticised them knowledgeably, and was soon working on the plans he gave me. For four months, more than sixty thousand people were employed, men, women and children, on restructuring the city wall, creating a rampart like the one at Shiraz, digging a deep moat and cistern, digging galleries below the rampart to serve for defensive mining and raising turrets along the length of the battlements. The walls were extended with small redoubts and defended in front of the moat by a row of small pits about eight feet deep and two across, between which were strong palisades rising a foot and a half from the ground. The citadel was repaired with sun-baked bricks. The artillery amounted to eighty pieces, which were properly prepared.

In the town there were more guns, which were distributed around the defensive works and accessible only by bridges. The bridges were, however, solid enough to stand the weight of the guns if they had to be moved to the ramparts. Eventually the Shah was forced to spend eight difficult months before the walls, whereas if I had not arrived he would have been able to take the city with ease. The many cannon which Mir Abi had got from the Moghul during the eight months of peace would be useless, seeing the condition they were in, if I had not managed to beg some artillerymen from the Governor of Kabul. He sent eight, who performed splendidly during the siege. But what I found most flattering at this stage of my life was that the Shah, who knew Kandahar through accurate reports of his spies, had no doubt that the state of readiness of the city changed completely as a result of my four months activity.

I shall spare you, my dear brother, details of the perils I underwent during the siege, one of the most bloody in this land of battles. There was no fort or redoubt which was not taken and retaken several times. The Shah's bombs devastated the residential part of the city. The citadel, resisting the early onslaughts, became the object of numerous furious sorties of six to twelve thousand men. The ground was thrown up by mines with which the Shah unsuccessfully tried to breach the rampart.

The siege engines also failed to pierce the walls. The army came to the fosse, at first unprotected, and then hiding behind carriages covered in coarse cloth mounted on trellis work. These mantelets had wheels and a series of long spars at the back and a strengthening of protective wooden beams. Each covered one hundred and forty-four men. With some pushing from the back, they formed a square of sixteen men across by nine deep. The Afghans showed their old spirit when faced with the fearsome mantelets, against which their light javelins were useless. Despite the gun fire with which the besiegers were protected, despite the musket fire from those at the back, they went out, torches in hand, and set them on fire without thought for their own safety.

In this siege I saw the Afghans as they have often been

painted. If they had been better organized they would have been invincible, and ruled the Persians for ever. I did not understand complete contempt for death until I witnessed it. Inured to hardship, they would pass the night in the mud, under the stars, or before the cannon mouths of their enemies as easily as in their own homes. They always fought *à l'Afghan* - perish or win. The Shah gave up the work of trenching because in one night they could undo the efforts of the attackers over two days. Their Nazachksis ran forward until they fell dead or found no more enemies to kill, and after overcoming the assailants in the trenches they returned to kill without pity anyone who had fallen back in disorder. The war was fought without quarter until the city fell. The Shah impaled those who fell into his hands alive. As to our captives, they were handed over to the people, who caused them to suffer a thousand insults before they too lost their lives. I would often try to save some poor prisoner, but the attitude of their leaders made surrender a capital crime. The Afghan people nourished a fierce hatred of the Shah, and these murders in cold blood made the sides irreconcilable.

By the end of March the Shah received a reinforcement of about forty thousand men, gathered from the region of Tabriz and Khorasan, where he had maintained them to support his coronation at Kasvin. He used them to redouble his onslaught on the citadel. Mir Abi tried a direct attack, with disastrous consequences. He was killed there along with the elite of his nation, and soon after this the Shah pushed forward his siege engines to bear on the city as well.

There was no means of holding the ramparts, and the withdrawal of the defending forces lowered the spirit of even the most valiant souls. Those who felt they might be able to retire to the lands of the Moghul when things became desperate started to ask themselves precisely when they should go. They withdrew from the citadel the goods they had deposited there. So as not to alert the people, who would have massacred them at the first suspicion of desertion, some proposed to join the Hazerai Afghans to muster those available to bear arms, while others planned to hurry to escape unseen. Udal, with whom I had formed a strong friendship, made me privy to his plans to leave and asked me to join him. I did not need to be pressed. I had lost my urge for vengeance a long time ago, and there was no hiding the fact that there would be no quarter for me when Kandahar fell. I willingly risked my life in the defence of the citadel while I could, but I also planned to stay alive, so tried to avoid any suspician that I was leaving. At the start of the sixth month of the siege, few defenders were still alive. The Persians, who held the surrounding country intimidated the populace so much by the treatment they meted out to those who fell into their hands, that we could easily induce them to help us. Gold and silver were the most portable items at the time. I had the thousand tomans from M. Norpéen and had added to it two thousand I had received as payment for my efforts and gifts from fellow officers who had been killed in the defence. With this I took the opportunity to buy small and precious items of jewellery. Udal had no need to do the same. He knew well that a display of wealth developed in the victor an urge to plunder. He had therefore hidden in his clothes, particularly in his turban, a vast quantity of pearls and loose precious stones looted by Ashraf from the Royal Treasure of Persia. That was all he wished to remove from Kandahar, and of his family he wished to take only his son, a young man of fifteen, in whom the violent schooling of the siege had produced a ferocity which his father honoured with the name of valour.

We chose to leave as the Shah was assailing the north bastion, which had suffered the effects of a massive mine. We took Udal's son Nehamet to the edge of the rampart at midday. Abdala, my faithful negro, a gunshot range from the advancing guard corps, hid in a trench abandoned by the Persians with our valuables wrapped up in Indian clothes which we were going to wear. Before leaving, we played our part with credit in fighting off the assault, which was bravely repulsed with terrible losses on both sides. Udal was wounded in his arm, but that did not lessen his determination to go. We reached the gate where Nehamet was waiting and there spoke to the officer of the guard as if we had a secret plan to save the day. As we were dressed as normal, he sent us on our way with good wishes for our safe return. We arrived without mishap at the point a little distance away where Abdala was waiting. We changed our clothes and before the following daybreak were well away from the Persian lines. In a narrow depression near one of their supply routes, we came across two slaves driving a camel loaded with wood. It occurred to me to buy this animal so that, with one of us mounted we should look more like merchants. But Udal remarked that the slaves would not sell the camel, which certainly belonged to their master, to whom they would be unable to return. Necessity forced us to commit a crime for which I have always been ashamed. I chose one man and Udal the other, and we shot them down in cold blood before they could cry out in fear.

After this barbarous execution we mounted Nehamet on the camel, which was led by my negro, and with no other mishaps reached the gorges of Zablistan in the middle of the night. We passed successfully through the Gourbent defile, where we lived on wild fruits for two days. Finally, we arrived at Ghazni, the main town of Zablistan, or Kabulistan as it is also known. Udal fell ill on the evening of the day we arrived. The wound to his arm had been badly dressed in Kandahar, but he had thought so little of it that he had scarcely looked at it on the way. When he decided to treat it at the caravanserai, however, he noticed that the flesh around the cut was dark red and lacked all sensation. He had seen enough wounds in his time to recognise gangrene when he saw it.

"This is the end", he said, "I am going to die. I die content, because I have saved my son from being butchered with the rest of the Afghans. I count on you to be a father to him." In vain, I urged him to get treatment for the wound, or if that was impossible to have the arm amputated, an operation I had carried out before and now offered to perform, but he had no wish to hear. A fever gripped him in the night, and three days later he died. Before he died, his father gave Nehamet the pearls and precious stones and told him something of their value. That immature young man grieved for his father but believed that with such riches he needed nothing more, not even advice. I urged him to go as speedily as possible to Delhi, where the Moghul then was, but he replied that he knew well enough how to make friends where he pleased and was brave enough to have no fear of enemies. He then left me and found lodgings for himself in the town. Earlier, I had given some thought to how I should handle this young man, but without regret I now abandoned him to his own wilful ways.

Here a break occurs in the narrative. Daniel arrives in India, without telling us how, and begins to put his plans into practice.

He then stops to acquaint his brother with some useful facts about India, later returning to the matter in hand, namely the conflict between Nadir Shah and the Moghul. To achieve a better flow, the order has been changed so that the background material comes first, to be followed by Daniel's account of his own experiences. He serves the Moghul Muhammad Shah, and fights the Persians in the Punjab. Nadir captures Delhi, later withdrawing to Persia. Daniel survives these reverses and marries one of the Moghul's daughters. Illness overtakes him, and he dies longing for a reunion with his younger brother François.

The siege of Kandahar had marvellously raised my spirits. It had convinced me that I had something to offer as a soldier in Asia, and being experienced in the face of peril I felt superior to ordinary men, whom I thought no more resourceful than I had been before the siege. I planned to go to Delhi joyfully, as if certain to be received by the Emperor. I would then approach the Court Nobles as one who believes himself their equal.

As I have done for the Afghans, I wish, my dear brother, to give you some idea of the Moghul Empire. Before Babur, descendent of Timur Lenk or Tamerlane, established his vast domain, known to Europeans as Hindustan, or Mongolistan, this part of the Indies was inhabited by people who came from Egypt. The customs, dress, religion and hieroglyphic writing of ancient Egypt, which are to be found among the polytheists of this vast region, leave no doubt about it. I believe the old religion continues in some of the most inaccessible parts. They worship a God who is creator and guardian of all things, and they render homage to their god without the aid of temples or altars, merely by burning the first fruits of their trees and crops. There are no bloody sacrifices, because animals, like men, are creatures of God and it would be a sin to take their lives. They eat only grain, fruit and vegetables. In the rest of the land, error and superstition have gained ground. People follow their priests in worshipping an evil deity as well as a good one, locked in eternal struggle. Only by sacrifice and offerings can the workings of the evil god be appeased. They have great temples and a priesthood to make the offerings, who burn incense at their altars. They are driven by fear, as more enlightened peoples are inspired by love and respect. They agree, however, that the good Deity will succour those who follow Him in this world. The cult of Brahma, or Vishnu, is also established in Hindustan, and is the most widespread faith. The Moghuls, for their part, follow the teachings of the Prophet. Strictly speaking, they are the Tartar conquerors, who came to the land with Babur, but the name is also used freely for all the mahometans who have established themselves in Hindustan over ten centuries.

Brahma was nothing if not a fine legislator. His ethical system is healthy, his dogmas a reflection of those of the country. One of the most admirable consequences has been the division of the people into four classes. Magistrates and doctors belong to the first class. As they are studious men, they naturally respect others of the same temper. The second consists of the military caste of Rajputs. Banians form the third class, who are concerned with business. The fourth contains the artisans. To prevent improper ambition nobody of one class may enter another, or take on one of its professions. It is this structure which permits commerce to flourish and industry be so general - a rich businessman wants his son and his grandson to continue his business. Membership of the premier class brings with it some heavy burdens. Their life is one of austerity and discipline bound by rigid laws. But this arrangement does not appeal to the fair sex. The climate of India turns the thoughts of ladies to love. A women who, after a few months of marriage no longer find in her husband the qualities she saw in the first two weeks, is moved to undo him with poison and search for novelty with a new husband. To mitigate such horrors, Brahma attached much value to fidelity, and offers eternal happiness to wives who do not survive their husbands. The same doctrine is followed by secular authority, and widows are considered to be a burden to themselves and to society. This is the cause of the fanaticism with which widows throw themselves on the funeral pyres of their husbands. It should be said, however, that strong governors now put a stop to this practice. Brahma makes the first class pay by austerity for its prime position. By the same principle of fairness he relieves the Rajput class of some of its social burdens to compensate for the perils of warfare. They may eat all kinds of food and have several wives. In the other classes there is a similar balance between duty and restriction. As different men have different characters, so they may take different routes to salvation. Hospitality is strongly fostered, and believers exercise it lavishly. Only within their own caste, however, because of the pollution which would follow from crossing the boundaries.

Such was the state of India, when Babur was forced from his lands in central Asia by the Uzbegs. Happier to encroach on the lands of others than to preserve his own, he established his empire in India, making his seat at Lahore, and afterwards at Delhi. No sooner was he there with his invading Tartars, than he set up a new legislature and form of government. All revenues of the lands were due to him, so that he could in turn recompense those who pleased him. The people, seeing that there were a million Tartars ready to massacre them if they disobeyed, were content to accept this arrangement; it continues to the present day. The children of the conquerors control everything, military, civil and in finance. Most influence and power comes from the army. There are two orders of nobility among the Moghuls, the Omrahs of first and second rank. Although by law neither of them is hereditary, few Omrahs fail to get for their sons an equivalent rank to their own. Only the Emperor and the great officials are above them. Former lords of provinces, brought into the empire by the successors of Babur, are maintained as vassal sovereigns of their lands, on condition that they provide forces for the Emperor, and maintain in the towns where they reside a troop at arms. These are improperly called their Guard, usually some thirty thousand cavalry and one hundred thousand infantry. These minor princes are called Rajahs, and are only minor in relation to the one they serve. The Empire includes fifty-three such kingdoms, and there is none which does not surpass in wealth or extent the richest province in France.

 The Indian military power consists of three parts. The first is the standing army maintained by the Rajahs on the Emperor's behalf and distributed about the provincial capitals. The second consists of the Moghul soldiers paid by the Emperor himself, dispersed through the provinces and defending the frontiers. Their true numbers are not certain, but on paper there are four hundred thousand foot soldiers and two hundred thousand horsemen. The third are the Rajputs among the citizens of the Rajahs, more than a third of the people of the Empire, because of their plurality of wives more numerous than all other castes together. Despite the riches of the military, there is also a lack of discipline and a neglect of fortifications. Grandeur and pride have blinded the Emperors to the dangers they face from enemies who would attack them. While only a quarter of their forces would be enough to vanquish all their neighbours if properly armed and commanded, they are never in that ideal state. As a rule no more than forty thousand good soldiers could be marshalled at a time. Citadels are peopled with women and eunuchs when a prince resides there, and deserted when he is away. All attention is paid to ornament, none to defence. The Emperor has a little private army within his palace, composed of women trained at archery and throwing the javelin, divided into companies and commanded by captains of the same sex.

In addition to these amazons the Emperor has a personal Guard, who are properly organized. Their corps was founded by Aurangzeb, and is composed of twelve thousand men chosen from six hundred thousand Moghuls. As a devoted servant of the Emperor, each Guardsman wears his insignia as a badge. Omrahs of the second rank have to send their sons to war with them. Elephants form part of this army. There are about five hundred of them, equipped for hunting and combat.

Their harness and hangings are astonishingly rich, and their enormous masses are adorned with splendid gold, silver and precious stones. In practice, this makes them more of an attraction than a deterrent to the enemy.

This brief account gives you some idea, my dear brother, of the country in which I proposed to recover my fortunes. When I arrived in Delhi, I was permitted to reside in the palace of the Sultan Noradh, former Regent and uncle of the Emperor, but I did not mix with those who paid court to him.

Without irritating the Omrahs of Second Rank by putting on airs, I behaved to them as if I were their equal. Nobody knew, or dared to enquire who I was, until after my audience with Noradh. When he received me I asked no favours of him, but merely said that I was waiting to hear whether the Emperor would admit me into his service. Instead of seeking a fortune, I appeared rather to have one, and a wish to reside in India with a position suitable to my station. I showed him the firman from the Shah which created me Bashi Khan, and the insignia of my rank as Min Bashi, together with the letters and orders I had bearing the Great Seal of the Sublime Porte, and my Commission for the establishment of transported families in the Persian provinces. I also had the Order from Mir Abi, making me Grand Master of Artillery in Kandahar. But I wished no more service of that kind, and moreover, I knew how the Afghans were regarded in this court, so held that document back. It would also have shown that I had borne arms against my former master and so cast some doubt on my faithfulness. I took great care to emphasise that I was born in Europe, that it had been my choice to enter the service of Nadir Shah, and that being born in a free country I had no other master but one I chose for myself.

At that time, Muhammad Shah, Emperor of India, had all the faults of a prince without experience. Raised in a Harem, surrounded by women and eunuchs who saw to it that his youth was passed in games and pleasure, he was at the same time ignorant and dismissive of affairs of state. Like the former Regent, he was manipulated by the Omrahs, who made him believe what they wished. The state was effectively controlled by them, and once established as Governor of a province they would give up communicating with the imperial court and became in effect independent rulers. The Rajahs only remained vassals because, hating and conspiring against each other, they sometimes needed to appeal to a higher authority. In these circumstances it was necessary for me to find a general who might want my services. After my audience with the Nabob, or prime minister, I sought one with Nessur Ali, Governor of Delhi and Commander of the Second Imperial Guard. He was the nobleman most esteemed by the Nabob and most hated by the second rank of Omrahs. The twelve thousand Muslims whom he commanded, and who were loyal to him, kept this hate in check.

It was worth trying to get support from a man of such capacity and spirit. I told him that my hope was to enter the service of the Emperor, but that I only wished to serve him under the guidance of someone as distinguished as the Commander of the Guard. The Omrah realized that I could be useful. He went the same day to the prince Nabob, and the following evening, having asked me to come to his palace he conferred on me the rank of captain of a thousand men, or Min Souba, in the corps which he commanded. I was only to have the title and the command on sufferance, because he did not want to displease his other officers by favouring a foreigner. The Omrah overcame this problem by creating an office of sub-commandant of the corp, which I was to assume on his express orders in relation to his own troop.

According to my calculations it would only need two years and two dozen picked men to train a Moghul army capable of sending Nadir Shah back to Persia. Unfortunately I was the only person capable of comparing the Persian and the Moghul armies. Already the Shah was master of Kabul and nobody in India thought that Delhi had anything to fear from him. When news came of the fall of some important city, he was spoken of as if he were a brigand who would pillage and withdraw, rather than as a tactician of exceptional courage and skill. As far as Lahore he only confronted provincial governors with their local troops. His army arrived there in less time than a caravan takes, and conquered it easily. I knew this prince too well to believe that he would be content to halt. At the audience which the prince Nabob was pleased to allow me, I made two suggestions. The first was to cede immediately, with the best possible grace, all the territory beyond Sind, to offer presents and deference to Nadir so far as possible without compromising the Emperor, and to escort the Shah back to the frontier. That would be a sacrifice of the moment, I said, which would seem less important with time until it was no longer embarrassing. I saw that many Omrahs with friends relatives or dependents in Bakar, Attock, Multan or in Waziristan would come out against me, as against a traitor. I pretended not to notice and immediately offered my second opinion, which was to retrench within and around Delhi. It would then be possible to go out and lay waste to the land between there and Lahore, so as to make the Shah's passage difficult. The Emperor could then retire to Agra, devastating the land as he went. The Persians, I said, will think twice about trying to cross such country if they cannot provision themselves. If they were to reach Agra, we would then be in a better position to engage them in a substantial battle. A detachment from the Imperial Guard could cut off their retreat by destroying the bridges on the Indus. The invader would then be forced to retire prudently, or risk a disaster. One way or the other, we should be satisfied. After I had finished speaking there was a great commotion in the Council, as everyone wished to speak. They broke up without resolving anything, and over the next three days the Court could not have been more nervous if the enemy had been at the gates.

    The Rajahs were all safe in their states, and indifferent to the plight of the Emperor. Of fourteen princes whose territory lay between Sind and the Jumna, one, named Jai Singh, Rajah of Ajmere, came to Delhi with twenty-five to thirty thousand rajput troops. This army was reviewed under the walls of Delhi on 8th February, and the two hundred thousand men of which it was composed generated such confidence that the precaution was not taken of removing the palace treasure to Agra. The palace was left as if we were certain to return in triumph. The army advanced for six days with no news of the Persians except that provided by a few fugitives. On the seventh we met up with enemy scouts and destroyed them. Another day forward and we were engaged in a skirmish with Persian cavalry. Finally on the ninth day, we made camp at Karnal, on the right bank of the Jumna, and commenced to dig in. We seemed to have forgotten that we came to do battle. On the morning of the 19th the Shah was seen to make preparations to attack our unfinished earthworks, and in a mass of conflicting orders we took the worst course and put ourselves on the defensive. The army was disposed in the Indian manner in the front of the earth works, all the infantry together without gaps and without supporting cavalry. The Emperor was in the midst of his Guards, mounted on his elephant. The cavalry was away from the lines on the wings, divided into squadrons so large they would not have room for manoeuvre. Rajah Jai Singh, who had been told to remain behind the earthworks, moved to support the cavalry on the right. He sustained the first attack and bravely stood his ground. On his death, his troops took flight, considering that without him they had no more obligation to remain. The Generals took this first setback as a portent of the loss of the entire battle, and despite the impossibility of making an orderly withdrawal in the face of the enemy, they sounded the retreat, ordering two commanders of the Imperial Guard to protect their rear. One of these was Nessur Ali, whom I was proud to serve as *aide de camp*. The two corps, divided into four more or less equal divisions, moved to support the cavalry on the left, as the Rajah had the squadrons on the right, and held their ground. We then made a charge, which brought up before the enemy's centre ranks. By means of a half turn to the right we swept round again to engage them, reinforced by a large battalion of rajputs who had stayed to fight in the hope of reward. The enemy, not understanding the General's manoeuvres, thought that some kind of trap had been set behind the earthworks. The sight of several elephants, whose drivers could not persuade them to move, reinforced this impression. Extremely surprised that they had not fallen on us, I commanded the corps, in the name of Nessur, to march to the town of Karnal, where the trees, hedges and houses gave hope that we could hold firm for some time. The Persian generals saw five large battalions, with cavalry support, exposed as if awaiting attack. Our bearing did not suggest a retreat, still less that we would flee in disorder. I recognised Bederned Khan, one of my former rivals, who came with a group of riders to assess our position. Making the infantry redouble its speed, I put myself at the head of a squadron of our cavalry and fell on him. There was a confused encounter and we retired in disorder. The Khan did not dare to follow up his advantage because Nessur advanced with the rest of the cavalry, and we rejoined our infantry. We had no more than five hundred paces to go before entering the town, and we were more numerous than the troop which charged at us. The hope of withdrawing with honour, after one last effort, animated us to such an extent that infantry in the middle and cavalry on the wings turned together and fell on the Persians. Nessur Ali was in the first wave. He was killed there, while I was unscathed, and by this turn of events would replace him if I survived. The Shah wheeled to the left where he was hidden from sight by a small hill. We owed our survival to this accident. With night falling, the Persians thought the Shah had retired, felt themselves abandoned and did not care to follow us as we withdrew. This gave us the respite to reform. It was easy to reconnoitre a route to the baggage train, which had pulled back to the mountains between Jenupar and Delhi. By the following midday we had joined them there. It was a hideous spectacle to see this multitude of men, for the most part without equipment scattered here and there without order or spirit and with the fear of death showing on every face. Sial Omrah, commander of the First Guard, was with the Emperor. He gave an account of our retreat with a sincerity and emotion which made me regard him henceforth with sympathy and friendship. At the risk of offending the senior officers I said that the army had fled, and that we alone had engaged the enemy. The Emperor made me go on. I continued with my account, praising the living and the dead, not dwelling particularly on my own exploits. I read in the eyes of the monarch and in the expression of all who were near me that this openness was appreciated.

"You have saved the army," the Emperor said to me, "The Omrah Nessur, who is now in the care of the Prophet of God, inspires me to reward you, and I give you his honours and his

possessions. You shall take his place in the Council."
At the same time he took a scimitar from his side and presented it to me. It was the mark of investiture as Commandant of the Guard. I prostrated myself and withdrew, according to custom, and was accompanied by the most noble officers as far as the tent of the prince Nabob. All the while they affected great pleasure at my elevation in order to cover their own shame. The Council reconvened. The Nabob spoke first and proposed that we treat for peace with the Shah. He was followed by generals and senior officers, and the resolution was passed before it was my turn to speak. I remained with the Nabob after the Council broke up. In a private audience with him I dared to criticise, with all the impetuosity of a man of spirit, an agreement which meant so little.

"To have peace," I told him, "it is necessary to be able to wage war. Things are no longer as they were when I suggested we encourage the Shah to leave by ceding territory and making presents. If we confront him with an army as ramshackle as ours now is, he will believe it a true mirror of our power, and will have quite the wrong impression. We would then make peace as if we were slaves pardoned by an offended master. But if the Emperor retires with the army, devastating the countryside, even Delhi, before settling in Agra, then the Shah will not believe he has made a real gain. Give me thirty thousand men and I shall myself face the Persians at the bridges they have put across the Indus. They shall be disabled, or if not, then turned back to the lands from which they have come." The Nabob listened to me carefully, but he was incapable of taking a decision on this matter himself, and I was not able to force him. The Omrahs knew the interests of the Shah. He had made binding treaties with some of them, promising to make them sovereigns in their own countries. I was sent for in the evening by the Emperor, in whose tent all the nobles were assembled. The monarch had arranged a place where he could listen without being seen. As soon as I appeared Darniven, the Grand Porter of the palace, asked me if it were not true that I had recommended negotiating with the Shah. Why, he asked, do you criticise today an action you supported yesterday? I saw that someone wished to trap me. Treating this man as an equal I berated him with all my might. "Well," I replied, "that was a fortnight ago, and it was not the only thing I suggested. It was practical before the Imperial army was engaged. Now it would be disastrous, and would cover with shame anyone who tried to carry it through."

I repeated what I had told the Nabob. "Everything will be lost," I continued, "if the Emperor remains another two hours in this camp. One day he will take you to task for not preparing to move." It was lucky for me that the monarch was in fact within earshot, otherwise I would have paid with my life for this insult. But the Nabob dismissed me with a sign and I hurried to withdraw to the company of the Guards, who already supported me as much as they had Nessur Ali.

The traitors carried the day. The same night one of them went to the Shah, who in response suggested that he and the Emperor should meet in three days time, in a field between the two armies. The unfortunate Muhammad, betrayed by those who had his confidence, put himself at the discretion of his enemy. Not having given his word to do otherwise, the Shah took advantage of this imprudent boldness and made him prisoner as if he did not still have the forces of forty kingdoms at his disposal. When the news of this strange reversal reached the camp, everyone dispersed. The victor would have taken my life if he recognised me. Having no more to do in the neighbourhood, I took flight with my domestic staff and about sixty officers of the guard, who wished to follow their fortunes with me. I crossed Delhi before the unhappy news arrived there. There I took four elephants and some horses of the imperial stable, loaded the giant beasts with what was most precious in the palace of Nessur-Ali and marched to Agra with the greatest speed. I did not feel far enough from the Shah even in that town, a dozen days journey from Delhi. I was now accompanied by more than fifteen hundred people, including two Omrahs of the second rank and a number of officers, who accepted me as their commander. We withdrew southward, intending to reside in one of the maritime provinces, in case the Shah should conquer the whole of Hindustan. I dared to hope for nothing more, but the thought of my ancestors inflamed my heart and imagination. I had heard accounts of the kingdom of Golconda. It had towns, arsenals and an uncountable population. Its governor was a mean and cruel old man, worse even than the Moghuls. I fancied myself master of his treasure, accepted by his people, obeyed by his troops, whom I would regroup according to the scheme I learned from M. d'Imberbault. It seemed to me that it might be possible to revive the former glories of the kings of this beautiful country. Perhaps these projects were too fanciful. That as it may be, after three months I had charge of a Moghul corps of four thousand foot soldiers and more than eighteen hundred horse. A company of Portuguese gunners, forty strong, accompanied me, and we took to the field with artillery and baggage. I was thus in a position to face the conquering forces, but by mid-July a number of messengers had come from the Emperor. The Shah preferred the solid backing he had established in Persia to the uncertain lustre of further conquests in India. Touched by sympathy for the Emperor, whom he saw as betrayed, he contented himself with taking the treasures of the Palace at Delhi; he himself avenged Muhammad for the infidelity of his Omrahs, ransoming them after treating them with scorn. As a result of a conspiracy hatched by them with the people of Delhi he had to kill a great number of inhabitants of that city. Finally, treating the Emperor as a brother, he conspired with him henceforth to keep the nobility in a state of submission and debt to the throne. This was what the runners were ordered to announce to the people, what the letters of the Emperor to the provincial governors contained.

My love and gratitude for a master to whom I had been close as no other Moghul subject had been, prevented me from considering the Shah's behaviour too closely. He dressed as generosity a retreat forced on him by the treaty between the Ottomans and the Emperor of Austria. Entering India as a victor, mastering the capital of that empire, he left it a thief and a brigand interested in nothing but loot. He punished traitors after profiting from their treachery. He afflicted the innocent as well as the guilty. His cruelty left an indelible horrific impression on the people of Hindustan. As he said himself, he was a scourge sent by God. The delusions of the Emperor and his Court in the face of this man were marvellous to behold. Muhammad knew how to profit from the terrible lessons of adversity. Having returned to the throne he wished to reign. His character, full of softness and goodness, made him acceptable to the people. I was received, on my return, as a useful servant. He confirmed me in my position as Commandant of the second Guard and gave me more authority than those I replaced. He provided from his treasury the fortune I would have had from Nessur-Ali, which had been lost in the pillage of his palace. Finally I was rewarded for the advice I had given, and for the services I proposed to offer. My zeal to serve him increased.

I proposed to train all the Guard corps in the most advantageous way. The companies were reduced to 960 men and I recruited senior and junior officers who would work with me on a daily basis, young men of high birth. In four months they were as precise in their marching and in their drill as the best trained European troops. The company became a battalion which marched six abreast in units of one hundred and sixty. At the sound of the trumpet they formed themselves into bodies of the size and disposition demanded by circumstances, without revealing themselves to the enemy. The ranks doubled, tripled or quadrupled behind the front rank which hid their movements. At the command to march, the first rank became like a bird opening its wings, without the least irregularity, leading the rest of the corps; and the battalion would form into a rectangle, broad or narrow exactly as the officer commanded. The skill of the senior and junior officers determined how the troop broke ranks, reformed, turned, split up and came together again. I have seen Europeans admire the speed and precision of these manoeuvres. Being well trained themselves, the officers had little difficulty in training the soldiers.

At the Emperor's birthday celebration, on 24th September 1740, three months after my return to Agra, I presented him and his Court with a demonstration of these new exercises. He honoured me with the highest award to which I could hope to aspire. I was made Omrah of the first rank, and received a present of four laks of rupees, to allow me to live in a style appropriate to my position. A fortnight later, the Emperor called for a repeat performance in the great square of the Mahal or palace of Agra. Having realized the value of discipline, he appointed me Lieutenant-General of the armies of Hindustan, with orders to the provincial governors to accord me assistance as military inspector - another witness to his high esteem. But I suspected that this new commission would be impossible to carry out, because of the old military men, set in their ways, because of the idleness of the soldiers and slackness of discipline, and finally, because of the tendency of the governors to have soldiers for nothing but display. I set out on my visits, however, with two thousand bodyguards that I proposed to distribute in the provinces with the rank and pay of Min Souba. In the Deccan I received a favourable response to my call. The Emperor also wished me to collect the dues which Regents were required to pay to their Rajah during his minority. These matters having been settled, the young Rajah and his mother gave me the honour of accompanying them to Agra. The princess, sister of the Emperor, proposed to spend the rest of her life at the Mahal there, the Rajah would pay homage to the Sovereign and respects to his uncle.

I was lucky with the princess over her retirement. Personally, I would not dare to try to persuade the sister of the Emperor of anything. After having seen her, however, after having had many times the honour of conversing with her, I felt desolated that her high birth separated us so much. My confusion and unhappiness showed, and she asked the cause. Oh my dear brother, what happiness it was to me when she enquired about my own birth! I could well remember the account recorded in our book, and here was a beautiful princess asking to be convinced. Of course, the book was not with me. She ordered me to send it as soon as I got to Agra. As you can imagine, she was obeyed with alacrity. I sent her the original and the Persian translation I had made in Isfahan. Seeing this precious monument to the fortunes of our fathers, this irreproachable testimony to our lost grandeur the Emperor undertook to correct the accidents of fortune. The descendent of a line of Asian kings appeared worthy to be his brother-in-law. The Monarch made me more worthy by virtue of the dignities he conferred on me. Governor of the Punjab and Lahore, Grand Porter of the Palace (or superintendent of the Emperor's house), and by my own wish I remained Commander of the second Guard. In this glittering state I have lived since February 1742.

After the loss of my illustrious wife, in the third year of our marriage, the desire to have my brother near me has increased as my ambition has dwindled. For four years, I have always hoped that fortune would again favour me. My state of health worsens from day to day, and tells me that soon I shall die. If you are still alive, my dear Jean-François, I wish for no more than that you should know you are, and will always be, in my heart and in my thoughts.

ADIEU.

ISBN 1412026776